Unreal Frontier

Christopher Lannan

ISBN:
979-8-9882721-0-6 (Paperback)
979-8-9882721-1-3 (Hardcover)
979-8-9882721-2-0 (eBook)

Table of Contents

Part 1

Chapter 1

At just eight years old, I get up at six thirty in the morning to get ready for school, my room already brightly lit as I fear the darkness. My imagination often gets the better of me. Incredibly groggy, I sit up to try to wake myself up. It was the same routine every school day, and I never seem to get used to it.

After relieving myself in the bathroom, I go back to my room to get dressed for the day. My legs feel like jelly. I walk down the stairs as if I am an elephant. As I stumble my way into the kitchen, I feel my stomach tighten. I leap up onto the kitchen counter to reach the cereal on the top shelf of the cabinet above. My parents would rather have me use a chair to reach that shelf, but this is quicker. I then chow down on some honey-covered cereal drenched in milk. After I finish, I make my lunch for school, which consists of cheese crackers, a bologna and cheese sandwich with mustard, and a juice pouch. After I put my lunch away in my lunchbox, I turn on the television and sit on the couch to amuse myself for what little time I have left before my bus comes. Unfortunately, my eyes just feel too heavy, and I find myself dreaming about a game I have been dedicating too much time to where I capture escaped apes.

"Wake up!"

A little shaken from the shouting, my eyes pop open to see my disgruntled mother. All I can muster in response is a somber "what?"

"You've got to leave now if you don't want to miss your bus! Have you eaten? Have you made your lunch?" Her concern also shows some aggravation.

"Yes, and yes. I'll leave now," I say as I grab my coat and proceed outside into the snowy winter morning.

"Have a good day at school! I love you!" my mother shouts as I walk away. I don't give a response. I'm too tired. I also hate school. School is the best place to go if you want the joy sucked out of you.

By the time I get to the bus stop, I'm wide eyed, as it is quite cold that day, and the snow is coming down hard. It would take a full-on blizzard to cancel school where I live. Thankfully, I don't have to wait around outside for the bus, as it had already arrived, and kids are getting on. I take my seat in the back. It's always very quiet in the mornings and the exact opposite in the afternoon. Although it is quiet, there is definitely more talk than usual.

"You think we'll get sent home?" one kid asks another.

"No way there's school today. I can barely see out the window!" says another.

The storm looks like it may actually be turning into a blizzard as we can feel the wind shake the bus. The bus drives slowly.

We get to the pond crossing. The pond is actually quite big and is more like a small lake. Suddenly, I hear a loud crash, and my shoulder is launched into the seat in front of me. All I hear now is screams. My heart sinks into my stomach. The bus is slowly turning towards the pond. It's not on the road anymore. My brain hasn't processed what happened yet. The front end of the bus begins to tilt forward and plunges through the ice on the top of the pond. Soon, the whole bus is submerged and slips beneath unbroken ice.

I finally lift my head above the seat and look towards the front of the bus. I see warped metal and the mangled body of the bus driver in the destruction. I hear crying and screaming. Water is pouring into the bus from the front, and there are leaks coming from every little crack.

Panic ensues. The kids are complaining about pain they feel throughout their bodies. Many have head injuries. Some are unconscious or worse. The water filling the bus is red. The bus driver has been ripped open and accounts for most of the blood spilt. Some of the kids at the front are bleeding quite badly from their faces. Their clothes are bloodied. Screams from broken bones and internal injuries can be heard. My shoulder begins to ache and swell. Pain shoots up and down my right arm. The water rising in the bus increases the panic. The bus is filled with horror. Yet, I still sit in my seat immobile, not making a sound. I am still in shock. The gears in my head fail to turn. What am I to do?

Kids are clamoring to the windows and the emergency exit door at the back of the bus. Kids are desperate to find freedom. Some try to smash the windows to no avail. Everyone is too battered and weak to ensure their own survival. The door and windows can't be opened due to the pressure difference between the inside of the bus and the water pressing in on it from the outside.

The water begins crawling up our legs. It's ice cold. If we don't drown, we are sure to freeze to death. I fear nothing more than death, yet at this moment, I can't bring myself to move. I eventually have to stand on the seat to breathe from an air pocket that is decreasing in size. I see other kids turning blue and shivering all over. It is at this point I begin to cry. The tears freeze up against my face, causing it to ache. The screams are met with gurgles as some kids are beginning to drown. Some pass out and won't ever wake. I'm advantaged since I'm an experienced swimmer compared to the average child. Those still fighting for life are struggling so much. I don't feel like I'm here. It's a horrifying sight. I just watch the panic as water begins to fill lungs. The sheer terror radiating from their faces could ruin a grown man's mind.

The air pocket is no more. Nothing has ever felt as hard as holding my breath in icy waters. I see nothing under the water. I feel my body fighting for me to breathe. I reject it for as long as I can. I finally give in and deeply inhale water. I am drowning. I have never been more scared. In my panic, I try opening the window. It actually pops open. I miraculously swim up to the opening in the ice as I continue to let water into my lungs. As I surface, my vision fades. I grab some stable ice to keep myself above water and proceed to choke on the water. I cough and hack until I can finally breathe. I'm exhausted and hyperventilating. I hear something pop up above the surface of the water. I look behind me to see a girl facedown in the water, not moving. I doggy paddle over to her and am able to push her to land. As I exit the water, I notice that I cannot feel my fingers or toes. It is as if they are missing. The girl looks dead. I flip her on her back and beat her chest, hoping she'll spit up water and breathe. I can't use any force, as my arms feel like noodles.

Immediately after my futile attempts at saving a life, I'm approached by a cop, who wraps me up in a blanket and picks me up. He carries me to paramedics. I see behind us another cop tending to the girl. She is tended to but not revived. While they warm me up, they tend to my injuries. I am crying the whole time and don't notice. I cry harder than I ever did and likely ever will. I hear voices around me, but I can't understand them.

I am later told in the hospital that we were under the ice for minutes. It felt like hours. The crash was caused by a sleeping semitruck driver. The semi reached around eighty miles per hour before crashing into the school bus. Only the very corner of the front driver side of each vehicle collided. The semi remained on the road, but the driver died instantly. No one else survived the incident. It's a tragedy that will go on to plague me with nightmares for years to come.

Chapter 2

When I graduate from high school, I am confused and have no direction. I decide to join the marines. I need someone to point me down the right path. I did well in school and have always been very adaptable to new situations. Teachers and school friends see me as one of the smart ones. They probably expect me to go to a decent college and achieve a high-earning career. Sure, I have done well in school, but I am still lost with where I want to be in life. Maybe I just need some time to figure things out. I still want to be productive and do something that can make me feel fulfilled. This is where the marines come in.

Admittedly, my decision is also made to help ease my childhood trauma. I still suffer vivid nightmares of the incident—seeing the children, many of whom I knew, freeze and drown. I failed to save a single soul. Whenever I would awaken from terror, I would feel like I couldn't breathe, as if I was still suffocating beneath the icy waters.

As I'd hoped, the marines are a good transitional stage in my life. Just joining makes the nightmares less frequent. Knowing I could be someone's savior is comforting. Trust in my peers also helps. Trust is extremely important in any facet of the military. I am lucky to be surrounded by those I trust. I have gained many friends and many skills.

There are good friends that taught me so much. One was nicknamed the Cheetah who's not only fast on his feet, but fast with a gun. From friendly competition, I have learned great speed and accuracy when loading and firing weapons. There's also the one known to many as the Bull who has helped me train my body for the most extreme conditions and help me attain great strength and fortitude. The marine corps has never been something easy to step into and it has taken a long time to reach a point where I feel truly comfortable. But I want to excel. It still isn't enough. I want to be more elite, so I've decided to try the navy SEALs. If you have trouble making it in the marines, the SEALs are not for you.

The marines trained my body well enough to make it past the assessment during screening, but not for what came after. When entering the SEALs, there is schooling, then the BUD/S training. The BUD/S training is the bottleneck for becoming a SEAL. During the physical conditioning, I have to put my body through training more intense than I could have ever imagined. The first couple weeks are not what I would describe as fun. There's a lot of running, swimming, and chaffing. This is all in preparation for the week known as "Hell Week." That week ups the ante. There is non-stop training. I never get more than two hours of sleep a night during that week. This training is made even harder knowing you can end it at any time by ringing a bell. The instructors tried to tempt us with it. They told us to ring that bell. I hold out and make it through. Not to say that the rest of BUD/S training is easy, but it's easy compared to the three weeks of torment.

There is an additional struggle I face during all of this. When you don't get enough sleep, you start to see things. I am beginning to dream while I am awake, only the dreams are nightmares. I begin seeing the corpse of the girl. The one that floated to the surface of the ice water. The one I failed to save. She is following me. Her face is blue, and her eyes are murky.

In training, I experience hypothermic conditions. I experience the feeling of drowning. Part of the training is to essentially make us drown-proof by binding our arms and legs in water. They'll pull us under the water and attack us when we are most vulnerable. It is all part of the training. But I continuously relive my past. I hear screams of children beneath those waters. Screams muffled by water.

I have an incident. While in the cold water, I pass out. I begin to drown. I am back in that bus. The children scream and flail in the water. I can't move. I see them all drown all over again. I drown all over again. I see darkness. Then that girl's face appears. I'm back on land, pounding her chest. When I realize what I'm seeing, I stop. She is dead. There is nothing I can do for the dead. I must fight for the living. I can't change the past, but I can influence the future. This thought flows through my unconscious mind. It's almost comforting.

I open my eyes only to see an instructor. He pulls me up to the surface and yells, "You gonna quit!"

I cough hard and yell back, "No, sir!"

I only passed out for a few seconds, though it felt much longer. I keep at my training, and somehow it feels easier. I'm not even thinking about what just occurred. It's much later when I realize that the nightmares have completely stopped. I'm not seeing that girl's face or hearing the children scream. I haven't forgotten. Those memories are etched into my mind forever. I am just no longer plagued by them. I am finally done with them. I just can't allow them to affect me anymore.

I have achieved what few who started training could. I have become a navy SEAL.

In my time serving as a SEAL, I haven't gained friends; I have gained brothers. These men are like my flesh and blood. They are my family.

I have my squad, and we always perform our tasks with excellence. When we are given a mission, we only ever succeed.

We're an unstoppable brotherhood with the ultimate skills for doing what needs to be done.

My brothers in arms may be my family abroad, but I could never forget my family at home. Sometimes, an escape from the military life is needed. We aren't robots defeating evil. We're human. We still have those we love that we don't get to see.

I only have one mission before I get to go home and see the family I miss so much. I make sure to let everyone know back home. I have a nice video chat with my mother. Of course, she makes sure to take up as much of my time as possible, as she hasn't seen me in person for months. Giving her the knowledge that I would finally be back home within the next few weeks has made her happier than I've seen her in quite some time.

My mother has always been this way. She hated the idea of me going into the military. I was such an integral member of the family that even I wondered what they would do without me. I knew I would miss them, but to see how sad my mother is whenever I have to leave for long deployments always bring tears to my eyes. The one thing that remains in this world that really gets to me is seeing my mother sad. I usually have a solution to her problems, but not with this. My dad, on the other hand, just told me not to get killed. He doesn't show emotion well. I know he hides it, but remaining stoic is more important to him.

Chapter 3

The fatal day has come. My small group of navy SEALs has just found a target's location. We've been searching for a terrorist leader who's suspected to have planned multiple bombings leading to the deaths of over a hundred people. Here we are, a mile from the compound we have longed to find. Now reconnaissance starts.

We don't talk much. We all know what we need to do and there are no better people on the planet to accomplish this task. Casual talk is something we do all the time, but now, all we have is focus. I know these guys all too well anyway. I hear about their families, kids, wives, cousins, brothers, uncles. They can usually go on about anything and everything. Things just feel different on operations like these and talk isn't needed to feel connected. These guys have gotten me through so much in the past and still motivate me to accomplish my goal in life. Maintain life where it is threatened. We all have that mutual bond and I would dive on a grenade to save any of them without hesitation.

After watching the building for a couple of days, we have nailed down the routines of everyone at the compound. There are fourteen people in the building. The target never leaves. Six others regularly leave to gather the necessities, always at predictable times. The last seven are all armed guards that have their personal patrol routes. They carry grenades and AK-47s. No one outside these fourteen people appear to ever enter the complex. We've seen high priority targets like this before and would not expect this to be different.

We finally decide to move down toward the complex in the cover of night. We carry silenced weapons. The patrols are all at their usual spots, and we take them out without any issue. We enter the building and see hundreds of pounds of explosives. It's everywhere. This is like a makeshift warehouse. We were never here for these and had no idea they were being stockpiled here. We haven't seen explosives move into or out of this place. Strangely, they aren't being looked after. The first floor is clear. We still need to check the second floor and the basement. Two squad members head downstairs while I, along with another squad member, head up the stairs. We see those not on patrol asleep, hugging AKs like teddy bears.

We incapacitate them quickly and quietly. A couple wake up and pick up their weapons as if about to use them. They are killed immediately. There are still a few people unaccounted for. I use the radio to see if the rest of the squad found them, but I get radio silence. My partner and I head towards the basement cautiously.

The sight is horror and the smell is rancid. The other two squad members are dead. They lie at our feet at the bottom of the steps. Their bodies are split in two. Their insides have spilt out all over. There was a trap set for anyone who came down here. Looking around with our lights, we can see many more traps lying around. There is a long blade responsible for the deaths of two brothers at least five feet long caked in blood. There is a light switch that can better show the room in all its horror. As the full lights go on, the true brutality of the room is revealed. There are many people: men, women, and children. All dead. They are on tables and hanging on the wall. Intestines have been ripped out of their bodies, craniums opened up, revealing portions of brain removed. Mutilation of genitals, bodies in positions that should not be possible. The terrorist leader was taking people from the village and experimenting on them for reasons I can't fathom. My partner keels over and vomits.

How did we not notice? These are recently deceased. Some may actually be moving still. That's when we notice. There's a tunnel. We didn't account for this. I think I know where those unaccounted terrorists went. We need to get out of here.

Then, we hear voices coming from the tunnel. They know we're here. I hear random shots echo towards us. We rush up the stairs and hear bullets hitting the outside of the building. I feel a burning envelop my body. My eardrums pop, and it feels like my skin is boiling.

Chapter 4

I wake up just outside the building. I look at where there once was a building which is now a crater. The explosives detonated. That doesn't make sense. How can I wake up after that? There are a few jihads lying dead from the explosion. I know we didn't kill those guys. They were outside the building, yet I was inside and survived. I can tell the explosion was enormous. There is a crater. It's not possible. My mind is hazy. I stand up and walk towards some bush and pass out again.

I awake at the infirmary. I feel strange. I feel like I'm dreaming, but I can tell this is real. Can I? I can't quite get a grip on reality. I just want to go home. I'm done.

I arrive at the airport to go home. The grief has overtaken me. I can't think straight. My eyes are rivers. My brothers are dead, yet I'm fine. They helped get me to where I am and I owe my life to them, yet they gave theirs? No. I can't believe it. It hurts so much. Get me home.

I get back to the local terminal. I get to my car and begin my sad journey home. I can't get there soon enough. It feels like I drive forever. The road is endless. Maybe it's my fractured mind, but it feels like this road could actually be endless. There is nothing but forest on either side of the road, and it feels like I really have been driving for hours when it isn't that long of a drive. I watch the trees. They are bare, as it is late autumn. I look back to the road and see blindingly bright lights. They are coming straight at me. I can't think. My mind is blank. I crash head-on with another vehicle.

I awake just outside the carnage. The cars are wrecked. They are twisted and mangled. There are a couple of unrecognizable bodies torn up in the wreckage. I'm not fazed. I sit in a stupor. I then remember my parents are supposed to pick me up at the airport. Where did I get the car from? It's not mine. I don't remember getting off a plane. I don't have any of my personal belongings with me. I don't remember packing. I don't remember ever leaving the infirmary. Was I ever even at the infirmary? How did I get here? Where am I? I felt like I was driving forever, yet all these events feel like they've passed me by all too fast. I don't understand. Am I dreaming? How long have I been dreaming? When did I start? Is my squad actually alive? Please tell me it's all a dream.

In my confusion, I decide to walk into the woods. As I look back, I still see the wreck as if it were real. I see so much detail. How is this not real? I keep walking parallel to the road. I hear an engine roar. I keep walking. I keep the road within sight, and I do not see any cars. I hear occasional engine roars. I walk for what feels like hours. I see no cars, but the sound of a car driving perpetually is lingering with me. I feel like I'm being chased, but I continue to walk as normal. I feel fear and decide to walk deeper into the woods. The noise doesn't stop. But then it does.

I don't hear the noise anymore. I don't hear anything. There is no sound. There are no signs of life. No rodents, birds, deer, bugs. Nothing. I can't hear the wind, as there is none. What's happening? I keep walking in the direction of where home should be. I think. I try to check the road, but I must have gone too far into the woods, as I see no road. I can't find it. At least there's some light in the sky. Actually, that's weird. It was sunset when that accident happened. I must've been walking for hours. The sun has set, but the twilight is still strong.

How have I gotten myself into a world of perpetual twilight? Although I can't remember the last meal I ate, I don't feel hungry or thirsty. I feel quite pleasant in my aimless wander. It's very strange, but I become at ease. The realization that I shouldn't feel that way puts me into a panic. I climb a tree to see if I can get a view of where I need to go, but I just see endless forest.

I remember my family. I miss them. They need to see me. I must leave. I can't stay here. But how can I leave? How long has it been since I've had rest? I lie by a tree and try to sleep. I don't feel tired, but I think I need it. Maybe it will allow my brain to become more functional and not feel so strange.

I fell asleep, I think. As I wake, I notice the forest is very dark. Lights can be seen in the distance. I approach the lights to see they are coming from the street I happen to live on. This is one huge stroke of luck.
I run to my house. The door is unlocked. I walk in. All the lights in the house are off. "I'm home!" I shout, not caring if anyone is asleep.

I need help. So many things are not right. I need reassurance. Nobody comes to my call. I search the whole house, but no one is here. The clocks say three in the morning. Where could they be?

I'm looking around my parents' room to see if I can find a hint. I find nothing. I decide to check the dining room and kitchen for something that could give me an idea, but as I leave my parents' room, I hear an eerie noise. It's like someone with throat cancer moaning. I look back at my parents' bed. There's blood all over the sheets. It's dripping from the ceiling.
I go to the room above theirs. I find nothing. I return to my parents' room and find something on the bed. It's covered with

the bloody sheets. I rip them off only to see my mother ripped open. Her chest cavity is emptied, and her face is frozen in horror. I can't breathe. I drop to my knees and hyperventilate as I weep.

This can't be real. This can't be real. I stand up and walk back over to her corpse with my vision obscured from tears. I close my eyes tight.

Then, something grabs my ankle from under the bed. I shudder and yell at the top of my lungs. My mother's corpse is now gone from the bed. A monster from under the bed tackles me to the ground. It's not large, yet it easily overpowers me. It begins shaking me vigorously, and I just yell helplessly. It's my mother's corpse. I close my eyes to shield myself from the sight.

I'm still shaking, but I notice I'm now doing it on my own. I open my eyes back up to see I'm still in the infirmary. I shake. I'm confused. My whole body has tremors. A high chain commanding officer approaches my bedside.
"Your squad is dead," he tells me. "You've failed your mission." He immediately walks out of the room and shuts the door in anger.

I can't help but to pull the IVs out and leap from the bed. I run to the door, yelling "wait!" and take a step outside the room into a void. I wrap my arms around my head, expecting to fall into an abyss, but my feet are firmly planted on something. I put my arms down to look where I am. The sky is Tyrian purple, and the clouds take up most of the view. The clouds look like spirits floating through the air.

Where am I?

Chapter 5

I gain some semblance of composure. I feel like I'm on another planet. I do my best to gather my mind and survey my surroundings. The ground beneath my feet is the same color as the sky. The horizon is invisible as the ground and sky blend together. There's nothing else. It's empty waste. This world is silent and motionless.

Am I dead? Is this my personal purgatory? Why the horror?

A voice breaks the silence. I can't tell what it's saying, but it sounds like my mother.

"Mom?" I yell.

I know it can't be. I have been fooled enough in this nightmare to know better, but there's a bit of hope deep inside me that I can't let go of.

She appears before me. My mother.

I fall to my knees, and my eyes burst with tears. She comes over to me and gives me a soft embrace. I squeeze her back. She is the most real thing I have felt since the explosion.

"I am here to comfort you, but I am not your mother," she says.

I end my embrace and stare at her. She looks exactly like my mother to the very smallest details. The short stature and long dark hair. The soft hazel eyes. I feel the warmth of her smile and the calming smoothness of her voice. My eyes and ears are conveying the familiar comfort of home all in her presence. Yet, she must be right. My mother would not be in a place such as this. What is this place doing to me? Where has my sanity gone? Then I notice something off about her. The façade of my mother's smile disappears and her true feelings are expressed. She looks like the saddest woman ever to exist. Her quickly transformed gloomy expression in the form of my mother's face tears my heart apart.

"Will you comfort me?" she says as she wraps her arms around me once again. Then, she whispers in my ear, "Help me."

Chapter 6

It's black. Everything is gone. Silence returns. I can feel that I am lying on the floor. I stand up in anger and frustration. I'm bouncing around a world I can only call unreality, and I feel like I can't get a moment to just step back and breathe. I want this all to end. I gather myself, and for once, I feel normal.

Then, I realize I have my gear on. I'm equipped like I was on my mission. I feel the walls of what seems like an underground tunnel. I walk in a direction, hoping to get somewhere.

I feel hungry. I truly feel. This gets me excited. Am I back? I see a light confirming that I'm in a tunnel. Things really feel different. I can't explain it. Feeling like I may be back in reality, I begin smiling, laughing even.

If this is true, I still have a mission to complete. I have to be serious. I can't let a vivid nightmare deter me.

I hear voices coming from the lit end of the tunnel. I have a loaded gun in my hands. I can adapt to whatever situation may come my way. I can do this.

I approach what appears to be the end of the tunnel. There is water at my feet. I look up and see that this is the bottom of a well. This well is enormous, maybe ten feet in diameter. There is a manual lift built in, likely used for transporting material. There's also a ladder that goes up the side. I silently make my way up the ladder. The top of the well is in what looks to be the basement of a building. The room I have found myself in is full of arms and explosives. This is a weapons cache large enough to supply a small army.

I approach the stairs leading up and out of the room. I creep up the steps and hear a television blaring and men speaking Arabic. I slowly open the door at the top of the steps only to see a man in a kitchen smoking. Unfortunately, he also sees me, and, in his surprise, he instinctively reaches for his weapon. I kill him with one shot to his head before a sound could be uttered from his mouth. I walk over and place two more bullets in his chest. Despite my weapon being silenced, quite a bit of noise was made, but there is so much more noise coming from the next room that no one was alerted.

I carefully peek into the next room and see three men. The men I see are just hanging out and having a good time together. That's the best way I can describe it. They are completely unaware that they could be in peril. I say peril because one of the men is the target we were after. I quickly enter the room and kill all three men. They didn't have enough time to know what was happening. I make sure to leave two extra bullets in each of their chests before searching the area for intel.

I instinctively try to reach for my comms, but I no longer know the fate of the rest of my squad. My nightmare was real enough for me to not know if they are actually dead. My head is light at the thought. I try to give home base an update of the mission through my radio.

"Who is this?" rings through my comms.

I tell them everything they should need to know.

"We do not tolerate jokes! When we find who this is, you will be severely reprimanded! I will find out, and you will wish you were never born with legs after what I put you through, you understand me! I don't tolerate pranksters!"

I have dealt with a lot of confusion after what I've been through, and this is only adding to it. I don't know if I can handle this level of mental manipulation.

"Sir, this is no joke," I respond. "I'm not aware of other people using this channel or any event that may give you that impression. This is very serious. I have intel from the operation. Please provide assistance!"

It doesn't seem to warrant another response. No help arrives.

I finish gathering the intel. This building was not well guarded. They successfully tricked us into believing the complex was the real base of operations when it was really a checkpoint. I leave the building through the front entrance and see that this building is in the middle of the city.

I can only assume the tunnel I woke up in was the tunnel under the complex. It had to have been connecting the building to the complex. That tunnel must be miles long, which is strange since I don't remember traveling that far to find the bottom of the well. Thinking about it, I honestly can't make sense of it. Where was my head at before I realized I was in the tunnel? I need an examination when I get back.

The trip back to base is actually quite easy from here. The embassy is also right around the corner. This place was right under our noses this whole time.

Chapter 7

I approach the checkpoint at the base entrance. The guys at the gate entrance give me a bizarre stare. They don't say a word and let me right in. Their reaction is unusual and unsettling. I begin to feel worse as many thoughts flow through my head. The mission was accomplished, but with the realization that I may not see the rest of my squad alive, it feels like it may truly be a failure.

As soon as I enter the base, all of my equipment and intel is confiscated from me. I am told to speak to the chief. My presence has brought with it an uncomfortable silence.

I enter the chief's room and see him sitting at his desk. He gives me a painful stare. His aging face becomes riddled with wrinkles as his face scrunches in agitation. His deep quick breaths make him seem as if he is withholding his rage. He does not speak. He only gestures for me to take a seat.

He stabs me with his eyes through an uncomfortable and awkward period of silence. The chief now red faced unable to hold in his temper finally shouts, "I can't believe what I'm seeing! You have some explaining to do! Where were you?"

I respond, a bit perplexed by his attitude, "Chief, there was a tunnel under the complex. Somehow, the target was able to transfer arms and explosives to a building in the city without being detected during reconnaissance. The target has been taken out as well as his bodyguards. We need to get back to the building and take care of the cache."

The chief's expression does not change. He seems a bit lost in thought as it takes him a minute to respond. He begins to look a bit confused.

"Do you know the whereabouts of your squad?" he asks.

The reality of at least two of their deaths starts to sink in. As I prepare to explain, I get an awful feeling. My throat hurts as the words start to fall out of my mouth. "There was a room under the complex. It…it was a torture chamber filled with twisted devices and traps. Two were killed by a trap. We have to go back for them."

The chief quickly stands up from his chair and shouts, "I am going to call in the marshal right now if you don't tell me what you've been doing the two weeks you were missing!"

"Two weeks?" I mutter softly to myself. "What are you talking about?" I ask in a shaky voice, hoping for some clarification.

He sighs deeply and picks up the phone. He calls the marshal right in front of me. I protest and demand, "Tell…tell me what you're talking about!" He simply doesn't trust me.

I am forced to sit and wait in the room. The marshal isn't too far away and doesn't keep us waiting for long. The marshal enters the room and tells me, "You're heading home early." That's not necessarily a good thing. "An investigation will be started regarding your claims and intel. For now, gather your things."

An MP enters the room and forcefully removes me. As I'm exiting the room, I yell, "Is he okay?" referring to my last squad mate. The chief immediately knows what I mean and yells at me, "He's dead and in pieces! The rest of your squad is missing! You've got a lot of explaining to do! May God have mercy on your soul."

I feel a huge punch to my gut. Nobody punched me, but I could feel it. My legs are weak. I am placed in handcuffs and transported with the marshal. The chief's final words are only followed with silence. Not another word is spoken. Those I know watch as I am removed from the premises like a criminal. It's humiliating, especially knowing I did nothing wrong. Nothing I say can gain me trust now. I leave with tears in my eyes as I attempt to hold back my weeping for my fallen brothers.

Two weeks. What was he talking about? I think back to my nightmare. How lucid I was. I can't get that experience out of my head.

Chapter 8

I was jailed and labeled AWOL. I had an extensive hearing to determine all I said was truth. The investigation took quite some time and threw my planned leave in limbo. The investigation has only now come to a close. I have been treated as a criminal for the duration of the investigation. People actually thought I could be a traitor responsible for the deaths of men I would throw down my life for. The investigation found my claims to be true. The last two squad members' bodies were recovered. The weapons and explosives were also recovered.

What I learned is that it really was two full weeks after their deaths that I returned to the base. I can't explain it. I avoided a dishonorable discharge due to mental health reasons. I am still being discharged due to those assumed mental issues. I've been apprehensive to explain the nightmare I experienced while apparently being comatose in a cave for two weeks. Maybe I really do have a mental health issue, and more happened that I just don't remember. I think back to the explosion. It was real. How did I walk away from that unscathed? After two weeks, I awake without pain or hunger. I experienced no atrophy. It doesn't make sense. I really don't know. I'm just glad I get to see my family for real.

Chapter 9

Getting out of the airport terminal, I see my parents waiting to greet me. My mother immediately comes running at me with tears streaming down her face. She embraces me as if she should never let go. As happy as I am to see my family, I can't even form a semblance to a smile. I may not have died on that last mission, but I sure feel dead inside.

My mother is oblivious to my lack of expression, whereas my father shows a face of concern. Something he sees in me brings a tear to his eye. Unlike my mother, the tear is not from joy. He wipes it away, likely hoping I wouldn't notice. He can read me. I can tell. It breaks me.

I try so hard to hold it all in, but I break into a spasmic weep. I can't control myself. The man who trained so hard to have total control over his body and mind is now broken. I'm in a public space, weeping in front of my parents. As embarrassed as I am, I cannot stop. I feel like a child.

My mother manages to become more erratic when she notices and lets me go. I start walking to the exit without saying a word. My dad walks with me, rubbing my back in an attempt to console me.

I just want to be home already. I want to be in a place where I feel safe with people I love.

Part 2

Chapter 10

It has been several months since I've been home. I started helping my parents around the house, getting groceries, and even regularly cooking. I find myself using up much of my time playing a lot of video games and watching movies. I've gotten to hang with old friends and enjoy the city. I've finally begun feeling happy again. My family is becoming less concerned about my well-being. My mother couldn't be happier and my father returned to the man I used to know, no longer concerned for me, but rather for the local sports teams. I'm happy to say neither of them feel the burden of my trauma anymore. They've carried me in my time of need and I'm glad to return the favor allowing us to be more normal.

I have told no one of my traumatic experiences. No one yet realizes that I won't be returning to active duty. They don't know of the deaths of my brothers or the nightmare I have lived. I was stuck in a deep hole when I first returned, and I was pressured into seeking professional help. I was being referenced to countless therapists who dealt with post-traumatic stress. I refused every opportunity, and thankfully, it seems I really may not have needed it. I wouldn't give that as advice, though. Maybe I did need the help, but I definitely didn't want to say things I shouldn't.

So far, it's all been working out. I have left my service in the past. Unfortunately, I have been a bit depressed not working for something. Everyone needs purpose, and I need to find a new one. I've thought about becoming a firefighter or police officer to help people locally. Or maybe I can go back to school and get into business or politics.

As it turns out, my hopes and dreams are dismissed by fate. I receive a very unnerving phone call. I wish I never picked it up. When I answer on this occasion, I hear a familiar voice. "We need you back here as soon as possible. This is an order. You will be briefed upon arrival. I made sure to be the one to tell you, as I assumed you may not believe anyone else."

It's the chief. Just when I started to feel happy again, I have to go back. It doesn't make any sense. Is this legal? The chief is telling me people far over his head are the ultimate decision-makers. He won't say who or how. I am just being told that I have to sign a few papers and I will be heading out. I never expected to go back. Admittedly, part of me still feels a sense of duty. I feel mixed emotions about the whole thing. I want nothing more than to stay here at home, but I feel a magnetism pulling me back to duty.

Ultimately, I don't fight it. I take the opportunity to redeem myself, and I say my goodbyes. It feels no different from any other time I left for duty. Maybe things can return to the way they were before that last mission. But that would be impossible, wouldn't it? My team is gone. I'm going to have to build myself back.

Chapter 11

I arrive at the same post I left disgraced. The country where I return to duty is far worse than I left it. The area looks as if it has been devastated by all-out war. The nation's local military has been infiltrated and left inept to defend its own country from terrorism without external help. I hurry back to base in preparation for what I can only assume is to come. I am not given the opportunity to settle in before I'm forced to speak with the chief. I enter his office, and he's having trouble looking at me. His head is incapable of turning in my direction. It takes him a moment to find his words.

"It's good to know you're back. I've always been able to count on your abilities. I'm sorry you didn't leave in better circumstances." He pauses briefly and then says, "Something has come up. The site of the complex your squad infiltrated in your last mission has become of interest once again. I don't know if you've heard, but there have been a series of violent earthquakes in the region within this past month."

I haven't heard anything about this. I listen tentatively to what he says next.

"The destruction of the area is partially due to the seismic activity. The country is seeing a civil war, and the natural disasters only add to the mayhem. The strange thing is that earthquakes have never been common to the area. That's not to say they never happen, but the magnitude of these multiple recent earthquakes would be enough to level many modern cities. Magnitude 8 earthquakes. One or two of magnitude 9. People are feeling them from hundreds of miles away. We have been able to link about half the deaths in the country over the past month to the earthquakes."

After showing me some background on recent events, he shows me the site of interest on an interactive map table. He then says, "The tunnel you discovered is at the center of the earthquakes. It's not a tunnel anymore; it's a ravine. The tunnel is thought to have occurred naturally, and the terrorist threat that you dealt with was just taking advantage of it. The major earthquakes have ripped the earth open about twenty feet across and over five hundred feet down in the deepest areas. The ravine stretches for over a mile. Some curious locals have attempted to explore the depths, but past a certain point, they just never come out. You were in this area before it split for weeks. Weeks will pass for the explorers, but they don't return. What do you remember in your two weeks gone?"

This is a lot to take in. I don't remember any offshoots or crevices in the tunnel. There was a cave-in due to the explosion. That's all I know about. I had those nightmares. That certainly wouldn't be useful information, though.

I sigh and begin, "I don't remember anything from my time there. I had a lot of very lucid nightmares, but I can't see that being relevant. I'm sorry, but I don't know what happened while I was in that tunnel."

The chief looks at me, very disappointed. He sighs and continues, "I was hoping you could be more helpful. You have been assigned to explore the ravine with some local forces. Most of the ravine is not visible from the surface. You will be conducting an investigation into the missing locals. Get settled in and get some rest. You'll need it."

I don't mind. As long as there is no gun fight. This is a rescue mission, something I'm more passionate about. It's why

I thought of becoming a cop or fireman back home. I strive to be a force that can prevent tragedy like the bus incident from when I was a child. Maybe more experience like this can help point me towards what I want to do when I finally leave my military service. I find the prospect of a search and rescue exciting, but I still have a bit of a mental block. That location only revives bad memories of mutilated corpses and a mystic world of confusion.

Chapter 12

I leave with some local law enforcement and foreign military officers. Some of the military officers can speak English and act as interpreters, as I am the only American joining the search.

We arrive at the ravine at dawn. There is a perimeter set up around the majority of the ravine with a regular patrol meant to discourage locals from entering. I say it is patrolled, but a couple people at a time patrolling such a large area doesn't stop curious kids from exploring the depths and never returning home. We are searching for the missing, and I feel like they're just letting more and more people go missing. Hopefully, we can create a way for local authorities to access parts of the ravine more easily, to recover the lost. There is already a primitive lift set up for an easier descent into the ravine. It admittedly doesn't look particularly safe, but it has been used to set up a generator and light at the bottom. The knowledge it could carry the equipment makes me feel a bit better.

After a couple of trips on the lift, everyone is at the bottom with a significant amount of equipment to help navigate the depths. The area has not been mapped, as much of it is not visible from above, and drones are difficult to control in these areas. There has been strange interference with wireless devices and radio down here.

Parts of the ravine light up as the sun rises above the horizon. Looking around the bottom of the ravine, we can see that it opens up quite a bit. It doesn't take long to realize the depths are much bigger than we initially thought. There is a secondary ravine within the depths that was not visible from the surface. The deeper ravine is at least as big as the one we're in, if not a bit larger. Shining light into the darker depths, we can see a series of cave entrances. This only complicates the search and rescue. If anyone made it down there, they could have explored any of these caves and gotten lost. The initial ravine is unlikely to have been responsible for the many who have gone missing. I don't understand the thought process of those that decided they should descend farther into the earth's depths. Most walls of the ravine are sheer drops. A few surfaces seem climbable but still dangerous. The climbing would tire even experienced climbers. I don't get it.

We set up a new pulley system to reach the bottom of the secondary ravine. A few military officers are the first to make it to the bottom to help complete the lift. They immediately head into different caves, presumably to start scouting the area. They were never told to do so, and I have an interpreter shout at them to stay put, but they don't listen. The shout echoes through the ravine. It could have been heard anywhere in the ravine, but the officers at the bottom ignore the order. They don't react and proceed out of sight in all different directions. The officer that shouted to them has nothing good to say about their disobedience.

We manage to finish the lift and get equipment set up at the bottom. More feel compelled to begin exploration without being told to. Our group is now less than half the size. Hours pass since the insubordinates left. I fear they may be adding to those who have gone missing. The one remaining officer, the only interpreter I now have, is livid.

It takes us until midday to get to a point where we can proceed with exploration. We attempt to radio in to the missing group members, but the radio equipment just doesn't work down here.

We hear bangs coming from one cave. It sounds like distant gunshots. Without a word, everyone runs into the cave. I'm left standing, still trying to decide what action I should take, as communication is not something the rest seem to be skilled with. I feel that I have no choice but to chase after them, but my pause allowed them to get out of sight. I just hope they don't end up lost. I hope I don't end up lost. Not far into the tunnel, there are splits in the cave, which means there are multiple directions they could have gone. The very first split causes me to stop in my tracks. I don't want to lose them. The caves have gone silent. I don't hear any noise. No more bangs echo through the tunnels.

I hear something. It sounds like a scream. It's not one of the guys I was with, as it is either a woman or child. It was high pitched and bloodcurdling. I don't hesitate. I rush into the cave with the scream. I have a snack in my backpack that I use as a breadcrumb trail. The screaming continues. It becomes progressively more desperate and horrified. I don't feel as though I'm getting any closer. I eventually reach a dead end. I really thought the screams were coming from this direction. The echoes are disorienting. It still sounds like the screams are coming from in front of me, but I'm staring at a wall. I am forced to turn around.

It's hard to see in these caves. I have a flashlight, but the darkness is thick. Despite this, I think I actually see someone on the ground. I approach to help whomever it may be. They are crawling on the ground. They approach me quicker than I approach them. They sound like they are in pain and dire need of help. As they get close, I begin to see a full view of them. It's not a person. I stop in my tracks, as I don't know what it is I'm seeing. This strange creature darts towards me.

I'm in shock. I didn't expect anything like this. I stumble backwards and fall to the ground. It grabs me with its front limbs, limbs that almost seem human. It climbs on top of me and begins a grapple. I try to reach for my side arm, but it's restraining me. It has at least four limbs that are pulling me closer to its center. Its center opens like a sea star, and bone protrudes from the gaping creature. The sharp bones dig into my sides. My adrenaline hits its peak, and I finally manage to grab my side arm. I begin firing into its gaping orifice. It leaps off of me and begins to scurry away. I give it a chase, but it's quicker than me. I manage to get a few more shots off at it before it gets completely out of sight.

I cautiously approach the corner it fled around. I peek around the corner and see it. It's motionless. It's lying in a puddle of blood. I think it may be dead. At closer inspection, I notice the blood is discolored. It's more purple than red. I flip it over to see it just has a large cavity in its midsection. The cavity is full of organs. There are no other orifices. It has no eyes and six limbs. It looks like a flesh blob with human limbs. I look down at my injuries and see that I'm bleeding quite a bit. Those large bones coming out of its midsection are like a cross between ribs and teeth. It truly did a number on me.

I tend to my wounds before deciding to drag this thing out of the caves with me. The trail I left behind works perfectly, and I make my way closer to the open ravine. Dragging this thing is getting harder, and I'm feeling weak. This thing's got to be at least as heavy as me. It's starting to feel dumb to keep dragging this thing. Then, I come to a split where I don't see my trail. I begin to panic. Have I taken a wrong turn? Then, light dies. My panic starts to subside as I see light coming from one direction. I follow the light and find myself in the dimly lit bottom ravine. I'm left a little confused. I got out of the cave much quicker dragging the monster around than I did running through the caves. I thought I went in pretty deep.

I manage to drag the carcass to the lift where I wait for the others to return. After a while of waiting, I decide to cover the creature up with a tarp that was covering some extra equipment.

A few hours pass, and there is still no sign of the others. I haven't heard any other strange sounds. It's getting late in the day. I have no choice but to head back on my own. I drag the creature in the tarp to keep it concealed as I get to the next lift and get in view from the surface.

Getting off the lift at the surface, I'm spotted by some locals. They show concern and try to help me as they see my injuries. I'm pleasantly surprised, but I have to deny their help. I do appreciate the sentiment, but I can return to the base on my own.

For some reason, I'm not too shaken by all this. I feel as though I'm becoming complacent with the unusual. Thankfully, there is a checkpoint not too far, and I can report in what happened.

As I arrive to the checkpoint, I see some of my people. They help me stay upright as I walk and are showing me a lot of care through the concern in their voices. My mind can't focus well enough for me to know what they're saying, but it still makes me feel happy knowing I can trust them. I feel relaxed. I feel lightheaded. My vision is fading.

Chapter 13

I awake in a hospital bed. A nurse sees me and looks somewhat shocked. She immediately leaves the room—a bizarre reaction. I look down at my torso and see my wounds were well treated. Despite that, they are worse than I thought. I'm chock full of stitching.

Of course, the chief walks in. He quietly sits next to my bed. I look at him in silence, expecting him to speak. He looks down at the floor, takes a deep breath, and lets out a sigh.

"Feel better?" he asks.

I smile and say, "Just dandy."

"The doctor that worked on you estimated you lost no less than four pints of blood. I can't believe you walked as far as you did, dragging that…thing. You were delirious all the way back. You were knocked out for two days, you know."

"Two days?" I repeat in disbelief. "I gotta stop going into weird tunnels."

He chuckles for a moment, but the lighthearted feeling dissipates as his smile quickly fades and he returns to silence.

"All the others that were with you never returned," he says. "This is hugely problematic since this country's trust in us is dying. Seeing locals vanish and an American return raises suspicion. Some powerful people are blaming us for the earthquakes and disappearances. We have no choice but to send you back home to help cool things down."

"You haven't told me anything about that thing I dragged out of the fissure," I say.

He is clearly not happy with my inquiry and says, "That abomination you brought back has been thoroughly examined.

It's of human origin. It's like…It's like Dr. Frankenstein set up shop down there and is conducting some twisted experiments to make an army."

My stomach sinks deeper into my abdomen. Could it be that I really did find missing people in the form of a crude amalgamation? Then, my brain finally registers the last word he said.

"Army?" I repeat.

"There have been more sightings of those things from down there. More people have gone missing. It's not safe here. We're facing hostilities from more than just terrorists. As soon as you are deemed fit for travel, you'll be sent back home. We reserve the right to call you back at any time, don't forget that," he tells me.

"Understood," I reply.

Chapter 14

They've given me two months at home, and I'm still not settled in. Not knowing how much more time I'll be given is disconcerting. I'm not being treated like any other service member I know. It's like they've created a unique role just for me. It's like I'm not a SEAL anymore, but rather some sort of weird government agent. The pay has increased dramatically, and all I'm supposed to do is wait and stay quiet. There is nothing typical about this new role. I think the chief is being used almost as much as me. People high up are using him to get to me. Do I let this continue? Every time the phone rings, my anxiety soars. I've been having nightmares every night since coming back out of those caves. I was the only survivor. We lost an entire search group, didn't recover a single person, and now I seem very suspicious to that country's government. Thinking about it, why would they want me back?

I see the news. The struggles in the area I came back from are well known, but there is different news of the area. There are reports of those creatures. Most people don't give any credibility to the reports from that country, believing any evidence to be doctored, as it's always limited and low quality. I know better. It must have gotten really bad if the news could spread this far. I wonder how many abominations there are. If there are enough, it's only a matter of time before sufficient evidence will accumulate. People are going to freak. What makes me more nervous is the reports of an increase of seismic activity not only in that area but globally. There are places nowhere near fault lines shaking. I fear earthquakes could get worse and kill countless, like the ones that have been occurring in the country

I left. They could even cause more ravines just like the ones harboring those creatures.

I don't want to go back. I don't want to deal with them. They're nightmare fuel, and I don't need to be throwing any more gasoline on the raging fire that is my worst dreams. Of course, just seeing a report of those creatures is melding them deeply into my subconscious. I'm unable to get the sight of the one I encountered from my head.

Chapter 15

Several additional months pass. The news reports indeed get worse. The number of skeptics quickly diminish. I haven't stopped thinking about it. Those things are all I see in my mind when I close my eyes. Even the darkness from closing my eyes reminds me of the caves. I've lost so much sleep. The paranoia. Part of my subconscious feels like I could be attacked if I ever let my guard down. I have to reason with myself to ease my anxiety, but it always returns.

It's getting harder and harder for me to believe that there is no threat to everyone here at home. These earthquakes aren't stopping. They're happening everywhere. More faults have opened up. They've appeared in East Asia and the West Coast. San Francisco has experienced the worst earthquake since 1906. It's like the earth is trying to rip itself apart. Thousands of people died in San Francisco alone. Half of San Francisco has fallen into the ocean. They were already dealing with one of the worst homeless problems in the country, and the problem has only been exacerbated.

Those filthy creatures have been spotted in every crevice that has opened up, including in the U.S. Not all reports can be verified, but I'm willing to believe them. Missing persons cases have spiked dramatically in those areas. There is too much lining up for it all to be coincidence.

The national guard has been ordered to guard the ravines and ensure no one tries to explore them. Likely, they may be required to ensure nothing leaves them either.

I've heard nothing back from any military entity personally. I have heard from people I know still in service that unease across the sea has increased as accusations of using the monsters as weapons have been thrown at the U.S. Could they really be capturing the abominations and releasing them into terrorist bases? This admittedly is hard for me to believe. I'm not a conspiracy theorist. But then again, I've seen things weirder than fiction with my own eyes. Nevertheless, I don't see those things as being easy to catch and release.

I do wonder how the creatures have been dealt with. Have those creatures tried to climb out of the crevices? There are no reports of such a thing. I wonder how frequent the sightings are. Most of my knowledge has been derived from what people have been saying on television and the radio since returning home. I may even come across the occasional internet article but those usually come off as fringe conspiracy theories. I'm feeling like I'm really out of the loop at this point, and I'm not comfortable with this.

Chapter 16

How long did they think they could keep this a secret? There is now substantial foreign intelligence that has been leaked to the public, proving the U.S. government has been using these creatures as weapons. They have not been killing the ones they find, only capturing them. They would electrocute them, as little else could stop these things, and then throw them in steel boxes. The boxes would be opened remotely once in the desired location. Of course, there have been a few unintentional casualties of war as a result, which is a major factor as to why this information has come to light. This is monster warfare. It's probably the strangest thing I am capable of saying seriously. But this is real. How can this be real? What world am I living in?

It also turns out that these creatures are in fact capable of climbing out of the crevices. That is something not even I would have expected. They have been seen on the surface on occasion. There's a video of one climbing up a sheer cliff face like a flesh spider. That one in particular comes out of San Francisco. Its movements are unnatural and unnerving. This is dangerous. Everyone knows what those things are capable of. They are known to be extremely aggressive. There is a strong military presence around these American ravines, and there's clearly a good reason for that.

There are no clear reports coming from the rest of the world. We know Chile is in chaos, and the destruction has spread through much of South and Central America. Communications have been increasingly shaky. The internet has been completely out for the past month, causing an enormous disruption for day-to-day activities. Phone calls don't reach across seas anymore.

Satellites have become impossible to communicate with. There has not been a clear answer as to why. It has been very difficult for the media to reach overseas in general. There have also been repeated power outages all over due to earthquakes. People are freaking out like the apocalypse is approaching. Maybe it is.

Why are toilet paper and bread always the first to get bought up? Doesn't matter the crisis; it always seems to happen. Panic makes people act irrationally. That feeling of panic is floating through the air as if a contagion. My mother has begun to fall into it while my dad remains skeptical.

The weather has begun to get weird. The sky has been perpetually overcast. Over the course of the past month, blue sky has vanished completely from view regardless of where in the country you look. It has been suggested the source of the overcast is from seismic activity that has caused numerous volcanic eruptions in the Pacific. There hasn't been sufficient evidence for it, and the expected mini-Ice Age has not happened, as it is 75 degrees Fahrenheit in mid-December here in New England. I now see the sun as much as a Beijing resident living in city smog.

All this is happening and I keep hearing my mother breakdown.

"What can we do?" she will say in tears. "The world is falling apart and we're going down with it. Isn't there something? Why isn't anybody doing something?"

I don't know how to console her. I have no answers. This is downright scary.

Chapter 17

Inevitably, I have been called forth as a specialist to enter the opened California fault. There have been creatures spotted exiting the crevices, but only very few, whereas there have been many more overseas. The creatures vary greatly in description, but the common theme is fleshy abomination. I have heard that since I've been home, the crevice I explored overseas has grown in size and completely swallowed the nearby city. The creatures in that area have been popping out of the earth and attacking the survivors of the earthquakes. There is no need to provoke those things. They are extremely aggressive and attack whatever they see, including each other. The one thing that is not exclusive to the crevice I left is the screams. People claim to hear soft screaming echoing out of the ground. No one is ever sent into these death pits anymore, as they don't typically return.

Now, I find myself in a situation similar to the one I barely escaped from while overseas, but this time, I will be better prepared with brothers in arms. The fault in California has turned into a flooded chasm that stretches halfway up California. I have been tasked with leading an expedition down into the depths and clearing out the tunnels within the Anaheim city limits. Anaheim is where the northernmost part of the chasm lies. We need to block off any possible entrances into the city that these creatures could potentially use in the future. To start, we are only going beneath part of the city and will bring more troops to finish the expedition if initial success is found.

There is a sister mission in San Francisco. These will be the first missions of their kind. If fully successful, more missions will be planned, going as far south as L.A., which is around where the chasm ends. Unfortunately, the entire span of the chasm is unlikely to be contained any time soon, as the earthquakes continue to grow the chasm and creature sightings are likely to increase. People living along the fault outside the largest cities will be advised to leave their homes and head for the protected cities or anywhere that is far from the fault. The outcome of these missions is hard to predict. The last time I went into an area like this, things went bad, but I'm confident that it will be different this time.

Chapter 18

We descend into the dark depths. The crevice twists downward in a way where the bottom is obscured from the surface in a much more exaggerated way than the other chasm I had been in. This chasm is much deeper than what I had previously explored. Its deepest depths are unseeable. This looks like an abyss that drops into the center of the earth.

We use professional climbing equipment to get ourselves and our other equipment to the bottom. It takes half a day. I dread the journey back. The bottom, or what we think is the bottom, is pitch-black. Even with lights, it looks like we're hovering above nothingness despite feeling the dirt beneath our feet. The air is very hot and stale. Breathing is difficult. There are tunnels going in every direction. We are tasked with barricading all tunnels and exterminating anything within them. We have to map it all out within the city limits. It will likely take days. We cannot leave each other's sides at any time. We are a team and cannot risk splitting up. Radio communications do not work, and we are cut off from the surface.

With me are marines and a few other SEALs. I've got to say, I've done some routines with these guys, including shooting, and the marines are the better shots. The SEALs are still elite, but seeing the talent of the other guys has boosted my confidence before beginning the mission. I don't think this mission will be hard, but rather tremendously tedious. My biggest fear is experiencing a tremor down here. If successful, I will likely have to do this routinely, as tremors could always open up new ways for things to make their way into the city above. I'll practically end up living in this place.

We select the first cave to explore and hammer a small metal hook into the ground in front of its entrance. A rope on a large spool is tied to it. This will help us not lose our way in the caves. In my past experience, this kind of cave system splits, twists, turns, and intertwines at multiple points. It's quite easy to get lost.

So begins our mission. Strangely, not a single creature has been spotted. They've been spotted climbing quite high up previous to today. It's surprising. Nevertheless, we enter the cave before us. Soon, we come to a fork. We are sticking with the left. Another fork. We stay left. Dead end. We turn around to go down the other path.

As soon as we turn the corner to head down the other path, the youngest marine yells, "I hear something! How did we miss it! It's back that way!" The kid looks like he still may be just a teenager and has way too much energy to burn as he runs back toward the dead end before anyone can react.

"Get back here!" a SEAL yells. "We need to stay together!"

We collectively run back after him. Confusingly, there is no dead end. The tunnel continues past where we were. The marine that ran off is nowhere to be seen. There is a lot of confusion, but there's no time to stand around and question what happened. We march on as quickly as possible.

We come out to an opening. We see the start of the rope. It is across from us, heading into the other side of the ravine. Everyone is paused in disbelief. There's no way it's possible. What we mapped thus far makes no sense. We are trained to be calm in any situation, but some of us are freaking out. There's a contagious feeling of paranoia floating in the thick, yet motionless air. They're acting like they're seeing things that aren't there and are jolting their eyes every which way. I can't see anything, but I do have the feeling of something swarming us like bugs that are too small to see. They're acting like they've forgotten how to walk and run normal. Moving around as if in a dream. It's also deafeningly quiet and my mind is making noise like sirens to fill the void. Things feel different, yet familiar. Reality is twisting, I can tell.

Someone else is missing. We've just noticed. We rush back into the cave we left. How could no one notice? I hear them. My instinct tells me to run toward them. I notice no one else reacts the way I'd expect, so I ask, "You hear that?"

"No," says one.

"What are you talking about?" says another.

My gut begins to ache as I'm flooded with memories related to when I was attacked by the creature. "Stop!" I shout. Everyone stops in their tracks with a couple almost tumbling forward from how sudden they had stopped. "The creatures we find can mimic human sounds," I say. "We need to stay alert." They should know from the briefing, but they haven't experienced it firsthand. We cautiously approach the location where I heard the noise. We come out to a new opening. The first cave entrance is no visible. This may be a completely separate underground fault. But, then again, it all looks the same. The top of the ravine has a lower ceiling. We decide to just head back to where we started. It pains me, but we will have to abandon those lost and begin barricading the cave entrances.

As we turn back to head down the cave we emerged from, we notice it's gone. The cave isn't there anymore. The rope is gone. The guy with the spool of rope is also gone. Guys are going missing right under our noses, and now, those of us that remain are lost. I'm speechless. The emotion in the group is getting erratic. Expletives are being thrown wildly. This isn't making sense. I feel light. I can't control my breath. My eyes swell. I think I'm having a panic attack. My heart is hitting the back of my chest violently. Screams. All I hear is screaming. Terrified and in pain. It's not coming from the guys with me. Our lights are dim. Fleshy blobs with spider-like appendages scuttle quickly towards us. We can deal with this. Keep it together. As the creatures get close, I can see these are a lot larger than what I dealt with. There's far more of them than there are of us. This isn't good. Of course, all the guys that went missing were the marines with their excellent shots. It's dark and hard to see. My peripheral vision is nonexistent with the flashlights. This is really bad. I can't concentrate. We all push our backs together to have eyes at all angles. These sick abominations increase their speed as they move towards us in the most unnatural of ways. We fire round after round into the messy flesh, but they do not slow. Some are dropped, while others get increasingly closer.

It all stops. Silence. We've killed them all. I stand upright. There is no sign of the creatures. Their bodies aren't here. My men all lie dead. I'm feeling light. This time, it's not anxiety. I'm losing blood. Lots of it. The lights flicker out.

I drop to my knees, as I'm too weak to stand. Out of the darkness, I see a light. A tunnel is glowing with a faint, eerie purple light. I crawl towards the tunnel. I feel compelled. I don't put in any effort. It's like my body is being pulled by a magnet.

As I enter the cave, the light gets brighter. There's an opening. As I come out into the open, I am dismayed by the sight of the twilight painting the ground as the sky opens up. There is tall grass. I fall facedown into it. I roll over to my back and watch the spirit-like clouds swim through the sky. The light dims. My sight fades away.

Part 3

Chapter 19

I awake in a wasteland full of purplish-brown dirt and dead plants. Aside from patches of grass, the vegetation is rotten and unrecognizable. It's a desert. There are thick roots popping out of the ground. They appear as vacuous veins that look either ready to burst with a mysterious fluid or drained and shriveled.

Dread sets in. I have been here before. This is where what I hoped was a nightmare came to an end. It looks worse. I remember being here vividly. The mysterious entity appearing as my mother. My confusion was immense, and it is returning. The anxiety is setting in. My body feels heavy and unable to move. Is this real? It somehow doesn't feel real. It feels like I'm dreaming, but I'm fully lucid. My thoughts and mind are with me. This isn't just a dream.

I gather myself and look for the way I came. I don't see it. I was in a cave. There's no sign of it. Could I really be here? I was deep beneath ground and now I'm above it. I walk across the hard earth. Maybe the cave entrance collapsed. Maybe if I find a soft part of the ground, I can dig my way back. It makes no sense. I look back up to the sky. I am filled with hopeless dread. This is not the world I know. I can feel it. My mind whirls with confusion as my senses cross.

I can't just stand here in a daze. I have to do something. I have to get back. I was here before. I have left here before. I can do it again.

I choose a direction and start walking. Time passes. Hours? A day? I can't tell. Nothing changes. I make sure to focus on objects that are roughly in a straight line, so as not to accidentally walk in circles. The only objects I see consistently are small rocks and weird roots. Nothing looks different. Could I be walking in circles? The more time that passes, the more my confidence wanes.

I'm going mad. My anxiety is reaching its peak. I'm not accomplishing anything. There is nothing but silence. It's furthering my madness. No life. No wind. Nothing. I can't hear myself. I feel my body pulsating. It's obnoxious. There's a dull ringing in my head. Small things are getting to me. My skin is dry. It's scratchy. I want it gone. I want it off. I scratch.

I keep walking. I'm not tired. My feet don't hurt. I don't feel them at all. They aren't mine. I can't keep on. I have no motivation to persist. I can't. I'm trapped. I'm in a cage. What do I do?

I stop to rip at my skin. It's not mine. I don't need it. I see a soft patch of grass like the one I last lay in. I lie in it. I look at the overbearing sky. It bustles with fast-moving clouds. The twilight is strangely bringing me peace. The cloud movement without wind doesn't even faze me. Maybe it's the ground that is moving.

I forget. What was I doing? Where am I? I don't care anymore. I feel relaxed. I continue my gaze into the sky. I'm complacent.

I close my eyes. I realize I'm not breathing. I don't need to. The ground is comfortable. I feel like I'm in a warm bed. It's no bed. This is a casket. This is my end. I open my eyes and realize my body has sunk into the earth as if it really is a soft bed with give, or more like a shallow grave.

This isn't right. It's too much. Panic. It's taking me. Those stupid roots. They're grabbing me. I rip them away. I begin ripping all of them up. They're all shriveled and dead. They are easy. I see a lively one. I want it dead. It won't budge. No, it is. I keep at it. It's moving. It's writhing. My hand squeezes the life out of it. It's pus filling oozes out. I rip the root apart, and it sprays me with secretions. It's putrid. I wretch barely able to prevent my insides from being expelled.

The ground beneath that root is opening up. Is it a cave? It looks to be falling in on itself. I dig. I dig as fast as I can. I need to get back. I'm filled with hope. I can leave. My nails hurt. They're falling apart. There are tiny bugs in this ground. I pay them no mind. My mind is focused on freedom. The bugs are entering my fingertips. I pay them no mind.

I don't care. I need to keep digging.

I feel them itching in my arms.

I don't care. I need to keep digging.

They're crawling on my face.

I don't care. I need to keep digging.

They're biting my face. They're biting my eyes. I scream.

I don't care. I need to keep digging.

They're in my nose and ears. The inside of my head is on fire.

I don't care. I need to keep digging.

The hole is deep. The hole collapses in on me. I am food for the worms. I have dug my grave.

Chapter 20

Yet again, I awake. Surprisingly, I'm not in the pit I dug. I find myself drenched. I'm at the edge of a pond. Things are different here. The sky is bright blue. The sky is clear. The area is luscious and green. The air feels cool with a warm breeze. It feels like a lovely spring day. There are colorful flowers all around. There is a farmstead nearby. It's a beautiful manor in a wonderous field of nature. I am filled with warmth at the sight I behold. My eyes swell with tears. I feel a calm joy encapsulate my spirit.

The term farmstead does no justice to the beauty I see. It's a luxurious 19th century manor on a farm that would have put most plantations to shame. On the other side of the manor, there is an amber wheat field that extends forever. There are animals grazing in flowery pastures. A herd of cattle, scatterings of sheep, and even horses dispersed in the distance.

I smile. My eyes gaze across the midday sky.
That smile disappears as I realize there is no sun.
My heart sinks deeper in my chest as I realize I'm still not home. I still feel some hope stir inside of me. I can't let it go no matter how bleak the situation may seem. I can find hope in just seeing something new. This can't just be an illusion of my mind. I can't be alone in desolation. I have seen another in this world before.

What could be in that manor? Who does it belong to? I can't believe I'm alone. There could be hostilities. I do not trust this place. It is designed for comfort and serenity. I see the beauty as a deception. I need to perform reconnaissance around the area before deciding what to do next.

It is easy to hide and observe from a distance. I just need to avoid the animals. As I move around the estate, I see a grand entrance, two side entrances, and a large back patio leading to the garden. I can't help but to listen to nature. The sound of bees buzzing and the sight of hummingbirds distracts me. I can't help but let the serenity overcome my senses. It melts me inside. I have to persist past it all.

The manor has three floors. There are many windows on all sides. Unfortunately, it is too bright outside to see past the glare in the windows. I decide to wait for night to arrive to gain a better look. I lie at the edge of the grain field not too far from the manor.

As time passes, I begin to wish for equipment that could give me better scoping abilities. I have none of the equipment I once had in the fissure. A pair of binoculars would come in handy.

I don't think night will arrive. No matter how much time passes, the sky remains just as bright as when I awoke. I feel as though I have been here for hours. I wasn't skeptical enough of the nature of this otherworldly place.

I have no choice but to find a closer vantage point. As I get off the ground, I feel a discomfort at my hip. I look down. I have a pair of binoculars. That's a bit freaky. I don't remember ever carrying them around, but I have learned not to question things in this world of unreality. I wish I knew I had them before. Did I will them into existence? I move to another spot and hold the binoculars up to my eyes. I see nothing. I can't see through these things. Despite something I desired magically appearing before me, I feel disappointed. I try to will into existence a gun…It doesn't work. I have no idea what's going on, and my mind is too fatigued to care.

As I'm pondering, I see someone exit the manor through the back entrance. It's a man. He looks to be early middle-aged. He slowly walks over to what I assume is the garden he owns.

There is a nice footpath through the garden. He walks towards the center of the enormous garden and sits at a bench. I am in a place where I cannot feel tired, but this man looks very tired. He's just sitting and relaxing in nature. After a while, he stands up and heads back inside.

I can't tell much about this place just from the exterior of the manor. I need to get a peek inside. I wait awhile before I decide to cautiously approach the manor. I listen and watch for any movement so I can quickly get out of sight if needed. I hear no noise coming from the building before me. I open the back door slowly and peek inside. It's a large kitchen. There are many herbs hanging in the kitchen. It looks like an indoor garden. There is a wood stove burning. There is an ice box. No fridge. There are no electronic appliances. It's like being in an antique home.

I leave the kitchen and head toward the dining room. There are lit candles all around the halls and room, only dimly lighting the area. There is food on the table. The table looks like it could fit thirty people. There's likely enough food to feed far more than that. For such a large table, I'd assume there are many people here, but I only saw one man. I continue to the foyer. There is an immense entryway with marble floors and a marble staircase that reaches two floors up. I silently walk up the staircase. There are bedrooms and lounge rooms for relaxing. I see a billiards room with a dart board. The elegance of this place is absurd. There is a door at the very end of the hallway I am walking down. I decide to see what may lie behind it. It is an enormous library of which I am on the second floor. It stretches down to the first floor and appears to rise higher than the attic. It would put any small-town library to shame. There are a couple metal spiral staircases spanning the height of the library.

I hear a door shut. It came from beneath me. I stare down to the first floor and see the same man as before. He sits at a table. Then he picks up a book he begins to read. I can't stay in here while he's around. Thankfully, this building is in very good condition and has no sounds of settling. I quietly leave through the door I entered from and leave the door slightly ajar, so as to make as little noise as possible. I decide to head up to the attic area from the main staircase. As I turn to go up the steps, I notice something from the corner of my eye. I turn my head to see the man standing at the base of the stairs. He is staring right at me.

Chapter 21

The instant our eyes connect, my core fiber feels fleeting. I feel like a balloon floating away. Then I sink like a rock as dread sets in. This is a new kind of dread. He is the first person I feel is truly real, yet I am far from comforted by the notion.

I find the will to break the man's gaze. I am shocked to see I am no longer where I once was. I'm outside in the garden. I'm sitting at a small table with a red and black checkers set resting on top of it. The transportation from one place to another hasn't fazed me. My mind is still trained on the man who is now sitting across from me.

"Hello," says the man.

I do not respond, as I feel paralyzed by the anxiety brewing in my gut.

"I never have visitors," he says.

After a moment of silence, he makes a move on the checkers set. He gestures at the board while looking at me with a grin as if to tell me to make the next move.

I look down at the set and move a red piece forward.

"What do you think of my living area?" he asks as he makes another move.

I take my time to search for any words and finally say, "It's very nice." I move.

"How in the world did you find your way here?" he asks with an interested gaze.

I can feel it in his voice. This is an interrogation. I can't tell if the game is supposed to divide my attention or comfort me into revealing more information about myself. I may be in a colorful garden with the most beautiful blooming flowers, but his presence cuts through all of it. His tactic isn't working. Regardless, he is trying to evaluate me.

I finally respond to his question after a brief silence and say, "I don't know." I make a move. He takes my piece.

"What do you remember before arriving in my… world?" he asks.

I make another move and say, "I was exploring some caves."

He takes two of my pieces and says, "King me!"

I look down at what he's just done, and when I look back up towards him, he's gone!

I'm not in the garden anymore. The light has gone dim. I find myself in an extravagant bedroom. I stand up quickly in response and examine my surroundings.

"Behave," says the disembodied voice of the man as it reverberates throughout the room.

I immediately head for the door. The doorknob doesn't turn. The door doesn't budge one bit. It's as if it's cemented in place. I turn back to the room. It's Victorian styled and has an enormous bed fit for a king. I sit on it. It is the most comfortably soft thing I have ever felt. It fills me with warmth. I quickly stand back up, so as not to be lulled into a false sense of security. I cannot be distracted from escape. I must leave. There could be a secret passage. I doubt I will find anything, but I have to try.

I begin knocking on all the walls, the floor, even the ceiling. I see and feel nothing but a solid cage imprisoning me, designed to look like a bedroom. I've knocked down all the furniture and have thrown the fancy rug. There's nothing. I rip down a curtain and look out the window. I'm on the top floor, and it would be a bit of a drop. The window surprisingly opens. I climb out the window and hang on to the ledge before dropping to minimize the fall distance. Once I drop, I topple over and feel the hard ground. It's too hard. I look to see it's hardwood flooring. I dropped right back into the room I left. I let out a frustrated sigh of anger. I look back to the window. It's not there. At this point, I almost don't expect it to be there.

In my anger, I pick up a chair and start slamming it against the walls as hard as I can. No matter how hard I try, neither the chair nor the walls show even the slightest blemish. This room is an indestructible chamber meant to keep me prisoner.

I don't think I've been in this room for more than ten minutes, and yet I feel cabin fever setting in. I'm more anxious than ever. That man fills me with uncertainty and fear. I feel like a trapped animal. I sit back on the edge of the bed. I stare at the door. I wish nothing more than to disappear.

For a bed that was the most comfortable object I've ever touched, it's starting to feel rather uncomfortable. I realize I'm sitting on my binoculars. I pick them up and look through them. My anxiety suddenly fades. I can see through them now. The door is missing. I put them down, and the door is still gone. I can see into the hall outside the room. I let out a sigh of relief and start laughing.

I gather my mind, as it seems I'm beginning to lose it. I walk over to the doorway, half expecting to be stopped by an invisible door, but I manage to pass through just fine, and I am now standing in the hallway. I walk towards the stairs extra stealthily and peek down them. The man is nowhere to be seen. I walk down the grand staircase all the way to the bottom. Behind the stairs is an old-looking wooden door. It is out of place. I decide to peer behind it. It is a stone stairway leading down into dank darkness. It is slightly lit by candles, but only dimly and not enough to see the bottom. I feel the need to investigate this place and head down the stairs.

The staircase goes deep, and after a minute of heading down into what seems like an abyss, I begin to question my actions. I look back up the stairs, and I can't see the top. This feels endless. I feel like I've already walked too far down to turn back and continue downwards. I hear crying. I continue down, and it gets louder. The crying isn't coming from one source, but many. It becomes a congregation of tears. Men, women, and children. It's all tearing at my insides. Then, a shrill scream breaks through the noise. I almost leave. The urge to descend farther has been extinguished. I still can't see the bottom. It's cold and wet. It becomes a battle with my will to proceed each step. I finally reach the bottom. I need to find the source of the sounds of despair.

The stairway opens into a large torchlit dungeonous room. The main areas of the manor are filled with natural light, but down in these dark depths, flames light the way. There are cells in this room. They are enclosed by iron bars. Panicked crying emanates in every direction. I grab a torch to get a better look inside a dark cell. I stumble back in horror as it becomes clear what the source of the sounds is. It's the creatures. The same creatures that have been found in the crevices in the real world. They are in every cell. The amalgamations are pretending to be people in distress. I decide to head farther in this dungeon. Thankfully, I'm not afraid of alerting these things, as they are already making noise.

I come across a table with shelving above and on either side. The table is bloodied. There is old dry blood as well as running fresh blood dripping onto the floor. As I take a closer look on the floor where it's dripping, I realize the entire floor is covered in a thick layer of extremely viscous blood. I look more closely at the shelving and see whatever is on the shelves is covered by sheets. Upon removal of the sheets, my insides turn to mush. There are jars of organs and limbs strewn about. Hands, thighs, hearts, and brains to name just a few I recognize. There are body parts I am not familiar with. I cover it all back up with the same sheets and move along deeper in this nightmare to see what else I can discover.

I find myself in a wide hall with archaic wooden doors. There are more screams coming from behind the doors. I decide to look into one of the rooms out of curiosity. As I slowly open the door, the screaming from the room turns into pleas for help. The floor is covered in fresh blood and meat chunks. There looks to be a mangled corpse twitching on a meat hook. The mass of flesh is crying in agony. As I approach with my torch to get a closer look, I realize what is actually hanging. A butchered woman is staring into my eyes and begging me to help. She's limbless, and her body cavity is exposed and emptied. She has no nose and has been scalped. Blood continuously streams out of her body. My head feels like it's swelling, and I begin to have trouble breathing. My thoughts are quick and segmented without order. I can't hear my own thoughts. I feel weak. I begin to dry heave. I look away. I can't bear the sight.

Despite my pity, I feel there is nothing I can do. I cannot heal them. Seeing how they remain alive, I'm not sure that I can even put her out of her misery. Then, the deity who is likely responsible for her torment is still a threat. Of course, as the thought of him works its way into my mind, I hear his voice. He's yelling at what I can only assume is another victim. I quickly close the door to this room in order to hide. The lady still has good use of her tongue, as she keeps calling me "mister." I can't let her alert the man of my presence. I don't want to become like her. I put out my torch and quickly muffle her so her cries become indecipherable.

I hear the man approach. He's dragging a screaming victim past the door. The victim is pleading with him. Their pleas are hopeless. I think we all know there is no convincing that man. The man decides to respond to his victim by telling him the horrific things he's going to do to him.

"Don't resist," says the man. "There's no stopping you from achieving your purpose. You will be donating to me all of your valuable parts. I will leave you alone after." He says all of this nonchalantly.

The fact I can't help these people tears at my insides. I want nothing more than to burst out and beat that unconscionable evil to pulp. Protecting others from evil is my job. As much as it pains me, I know I'm not capable. I am powerless. I'm having trouble stopping myself from weeping as I continue to gag the tortured woman. I don't want to be here. I'd rather be lost in the wastes of this world.

He does eventually pass, and I no longer hear the wails of his newest victim as others now drown them out. I remain frozen. I don't want to leave.

I realize I'm still muffling the lady. I gather myself and force my emotions down so I can leave the woman behind. I continue down the hall toward where the newest victim was dragged. There are even more stairs heading down. I feel that there is nothing left to do but proceed farther into the depths.

It doesn't take long before I reach the bottom. There is a large gilded wooden door. It's cracked open, so I peer in. The room is brightly lit with many candles. There is a large desk with drawers. Above the desk is a large decayed painting of a small farmstead. On the desk is a large book. I proceed into the room and skim through the book. It appears to be a lab book full of descriptions of experiments. There's a lot of content to go through, so I hold on to it as I continue to search the room. I rummage through the desk and find a small journal. This I can't skim through, as it has a lock keeping it closed. The only other things in the desk are drawings and scribbles of a madman. Some notes are just one-word scribbles that say things like "GO," "TAKE," or "MOVE." Some say, "DO IT!" A couple say something interesting. I find a note saying "Remember" and "Don't forget." I wish I had something to put this all in. Just as the thought enters my mind, I kick something as I move my feet back toward the door. It's an empty bag. It looks fairly modern and doesn't fit the aesthetics of this place. I stuff all that I can into the bag.

I hear him! He's yelling!

"WHERE ARE YOU? I WILL GET YOU! YOU WILL BE MY BEST EXPERIMENT! I WILL CONQUER!"

He's found out! He knows I'm here! I need to escape! But this is a dead end! Then I see it. It's a trapdoor! I open it and jump in without even looking. I expected to drop into somewhere, but I'm still falling. There's no air resistance. It's pitch-black. I feel like a blind man floating through space.

Minutes pass. I have no senses other than touch. I can feel myself. I can feel the bag I'm carrying. I would examine my findings, but I can't see. Then, I do. There is a light in front of me. I realize I'm not falling. There is ground beneath my feet. I head towards the light. I make it to the opening and see a familiar place. I'm back where I started.

The sky is purple. The ground is too. I'm back in the strange wasteland that drove me crazy. Yet, I feel relieved. I see a lone bare tree. I don't remember seeing anything like it before.

I walk towards it and sit at its base. I do not know what I should do next, but maybe the writings of a madman can somehow help.

Chapter 22

I sit for a while. I need to collect my mind and think. I need to know more about this place and how to leave. Unfortunately, the ravings of a lunatic are my only option. I open the book I stole from him. It appears to be a lab book full of experiments. The goal of these experiments is clearly stated, and I'm not sure how to feel about it. The goal is simply stated in one word: "Leave." Is he real? Is he not from this world? Then why is he still here? His weird demons seem to be getting to the real world just fine. Heck, I've left this world, although I'm still completely lost as to how.

The beginning of this lab book seems innocent. He didn't begin with test subjects; then again, how could he get test subjects if he didn't even know how to get back to the real world? The beginning of the book goes into what I have become familiar with, the dream-like feeling of this world. He makes it seem more like a dream than I had imagined. In one passage, he states, "This world is like a dream where you are aware of one's own slumber. It is possible to manipulate how this world presents itself to me once the mind becomes well attuned to the unreality."

He declares that his strong desire for the real world has allowed him to develop rifts between this world and ours. He repeatedly refers to the worlds as reality and unreality. It's a bit weird because I had the same word in my head. If his mind has truly had influence over this world, then maybe he had influence over me. Getting back to these rifts, he makes the statement that things could move from reality to unreality but not the other way around. He also says it takes an immense amount of energy to make a rift. In a world he says he cannot die or ever be sick in, he feels that he loses a part of himself whenever he makes a rift.

Not only that, just the sheer amount of time stuck here has taken a toll on him. His mind and this world are directly connected and are influencing each other.

Regardless of the effects these experiments had on his well-being, he continued his pursuit of escape. The first experiments he conducted with these rifts dealt with finding optimal locations for them. He states, "The rifts can only be formed in complete darkness. Underground is the best option for allowing the power of choice over the location."

Due to the location restriction, he was mostly able to bring subterranean creatures to this world like some rodents and bugs. Interacting with real creatures brought him endless excitement and further motivated him. Unfortunately, his next experiments were conducted on said creatures. He tried forcing them back to the real world, a task he was unable to achieve himself. Herein lies the problem: he found success, but the creatures returned to the real world as mangled carcasses. The flesh of the animals was rearranged in a horrifying manner, and the bugs were completely unrecognizable.

This is where the experiments seemed to get far worse. Sick thoughts drifted through this man's mind. Out of curiosity, he decided to simulate the rearrangement of flesh that these animals would experience by traveling through a rift while still in unreality. In unreality, these animals do not die. No matter what he did to them, they were still kicking. After sending already mutilated rodent bodies through these rifts, he found a method of "reconfiguring" their bodies to survive the trip back to the real world. The side effect of the so-called "reconfiguration" is that it makes the animals act rabid and incredibly aggressive to everything, including each other. They had to be kept separate to prevent them from ripping each other apart.

Rather than looking for more reasonable traversal through these rifts, he instead focused on placing the rifts more strategically to gather other animals. According to his book, he managed to capture a bear. He said he was able to warp the animal to "perfection." This bear was captured from a cavern, experimented on, and then sent back to that same cavern. Strangely, it did keep some semblance of being a bear and would return to the cavern it was initially abducted from. The rift stayed, and it would move between realities as it pleased, to the psycho's pleasant surprise.

His madness seems to accelerate. The deeper down the rabbit hole he explores, the quicker his mind seems to decline. I don't think escape is on his mind anymore. He believes his understanding of this world has grown to a level where he had begun to feel like a god. There is much he has learned about controlling this world that he has not documented. I assume he hasn't needed these experiments for most of his current abilities. Yet, he persists.

I have reached the part of the book where he has gotten to abducting people. He has conquered this world, but to him, it's not real and therefore meaningless. The power has gone to his head. He doesn't believe he can achieve any more here. He wants to conquer the real world. The next experiments are conducted on human beings. He made soldiers to invade the real world. He makes the claim that he will somehow unite the two worlds together and take control of everything. I don't understand how that could be possible, but I need to make sure it doesn't happen.

Delving further into the human experiments, he has found that humans are actually easy "prey." Using words like this, he has a full understanding of the evil he harbors. He has found that humans are easily tempted by curiosity. His influence over people's minds can reach out through the rifts. He gives people the desire to approach unreality to become his subjects. This has led to the man discovering that these rifts are not singular points in space, but rather that "the rift is more of a slow bleed of unreality seeping into reality." The area around these rifts is a mixing of both worlds.

Up to this point, there have been no images of his experiments, but now they are appearing. There are dozens of detailed images depicting the process of turning real people into horrible abominations. Living people being split and morphed together or separated into new unique organisms. At no point in the process does it appear they are not alive despite the tremendous modifications they undergo. I feel that I can hear the screams of these people just from looking at the pictures. No, I do hear them. It's loud, deafening. I feel my heart rise to my throat and tears well up in my eyes. I can't keep looking at this. I can't even understand what he's writing anymore. It's unreadable. All he's doing is ripping people apart so he can put them back together in a form that can be a hyper-aggressive, mindless soldier.

I angrily toss the book far from where I'm sitting. I can't say reading that book was very useful. It was disgusting and morbid by the end. The amount of grotesque detail in the human experiments is more than I can handle.

But what else can I do? I reach for the journal, hoping to finally get some more useful information. There was a lot he learned that he never wrote about in that book. I just want to glean a hint of something that is more useful than a one-way rift. Looking at it closer, I realized it's locked. The thing is like stone and won't bend or budge. Of course, he made it impossible to open. I sit and contemplate.

Chapter 23

After sitting for an indiscernible amount of time, I decide I should at least keep the lab book with me. I approach where I tossed the book and see it has sunk into the ground. As I pick it up, I see a hole start to form where it once lay. The dirt is falling into a pit, which quickly grows. I stumble backward as my foot becomes stuck in it. The hole continues to grow, and I find myself falling into a sinkhole. With an ungraceful thud, I fall through the ground into a cave lit by the hole now above my head.

I get back on my feet immediately. The change in my surroundings fills me with hope. I never thought I would be this excited to be back in a cave. I entered this world through a cave, so maybe I can exit through one. I know what that lab book said about the rifts, but I've left before, and I should be able to do it again. I don't have any other option anyway. The only alternative I can see is to wait around for the madman to find me. I march on and explore the cave.

The cave opens up to a large, roofed chasm dripping with streaks of water, glistening like crystals. Stalactites and stalagmites dot the entirety of the chasm. There is what appears to be an enormous naturally occurring fountain at the center. Of course, it can't be natural. Nothing in this world is. There is nothing this magnificent in appearance occurring naturally in the real world.

I approach the fountain and peer into the highly reflective glistening waters. I see my face staring back at me. I would think that after everything I've been through, I would look roughed up, but I look no worse for wear. This water certainly doesn't reflect how I feel. As I stare into the water, I notice some movement in the reflection. Someone is behind me. It's my mother!

Without turning around, I yell, "What are you?"

She recoils back in surprise as if I am not the one who's supposed to be surprised. She says, "I'm sorry. I thought this appearance would bring you comfort. I will change to my preferred form if you'd like to see me as I normally am."

She then shifts her form to a younger woman of a very different appearance. Watching the quick transformation through the water's reflection makes my heart jump, and I quickly turn around to stare directly at her. I now see a very warm but apprehensive smile from a gentle face.

Strangely, I'm starting to feel bad for startling her despite that she's the one who startled me in the first place.

"Who are you?" I ask in a demanding voice. I still do not trust the entity presenting itself before me.

"I may not be your mother, but I am *a* mother," she says. "I gave birth to the world you find yourself in."

"You're not a very good mother," I reply only somewhat in jest.

She reciprocates my comment with a large frown. She winces a bit as if pained by the statement. She tears up and replies, "I'm truly not a very good mother. I apologize. I have tried my best and made mistakes. I have learned and I am still learning. But I still haven't learned enough to deal with my troubles. I need help."

I'm not sure how to process this. This is very different from the last conversation I had, as that was with a man with no sanity remaining in his mind. I still don't trust what is unfolding in front of my eyes. After a brief pause, I finally say, "Do you really expect me to help? I don't think there is anything I could do even if I trusted you. If this is your world, you should be able to help yourself."

She begins to cry and collapses to her knees. In her groveling, she cries, "I can't do it. I haven't had control of my world for such a long time. There is nothing more I can do. But you can. You're human. Your mind works. Mine doesn't. It's different. Please. Your world will be lost like mine if I don't get help." She's panicking.

Maybe it's the human side to me, but she's beginning to break through to me. I built my life around helping those in need. I can't tell for sure if she's serious, but my heart cracks at the sight of this woman.

"Okay," I reply. "But you have a lot of explaining to do."

Chapter 24

The woman begins to smile, and her tears fade. The woman then says in the sincerest tone, "Thank you…Please ask whatever you'd like. It may seem we have all eternity, but I can assure you that we do not."

"What exactly are you?" I ask.

"I am the mother of this world, as I told you," she replies, seemingly confused by the question.

"But you look like an ordinary person," I respond.

"I don't have any one form," she says. "I chose to appear as what I believed mother nature would look like. There are many depictions of mother earth and mother nature in your world. There are many cultures with gods and goddesses, which I looked to for influence. I really admire it all."

"How do you know about all that? How do you know about my mother?" I ask.

"I have long been able to see into your world," she stated. "I have watched over mankind for a thousand years and revered it deeply. I love it dearly and have always wished to reach out to your world. The problems came when I succeeded."

"What do you mean?" I ask.

"It must have been a couple hundred years ago. It was then when I finally found a way to reach out to your world. I did something unforgivable. I stole someone." As she finishes saying this, her eyes well up. "That someone had a life, which I was closely observing. I grew jealous of those around this person. I decided my first interaction with your world would be to steal the person I grew to desire." She pauses for a moment to collect herself. "That person had a life and a family. I took it from them."

"I don't think I'll like your answer, but what happened to them?" I ask.

"You've already met," she says.

Of course. I feel like it was the only possibility. That mad Dr. Frankenstein is the one she's referring to.

"How do you fall for that monster?" I ask, bewildered.

"He wasn't always like this," she responds. "I made him into what he is today by trapping him here. He went mad long ago during his countless attempts of escape. My jealousy faded once the gravity of my actions sank in. I wanted nothing more but for him to return to his true loved ones, but I failed to achieve that for him." Her speech began to quiver with her last few words. Tears are rolling down her face as she struggles to maintain composure.

For some reason, I suddenly remember seeing her before. It was the last time I came to this world, just before I went back to the real world.

"I saw you," I say. "I was here before, and after seeing you, I was back in the real world. How did I get back to reality last time?"

"I wanted to send you back," she responds. "I'm sorry our first interaction couldn't have been under better circumstances. I was in a panic, fleeing the man's madness. I asked for your help before you went back to your world to get the help I needed. Your world needed to be prepared. Now, I'm in a more stable mentality, and the man is unaware of a way to get to me."

"If you can send me back, then why didn't you send him back?" I ask.

"I didn't know how at the time," she says. "In fact, I learned how from the man we're hiding from. As he stayed in my world, his knowledge grew as fast as his madness. He has mastered this realm, and I have not. The human mind has shown to have so much potential here. He is able to leave this world seamlessly, while it takes an incredible amount of energy for me to send anything to the real world."

"Wait…If he could leave and being here brought him madness…I'm not connecting the dots here," I say, confused.

"He had already gone completely mad by the time he discovered how to travel between our worlds," she says. "I only know of a single time he returned to your world. He fled back here upon realizing his power only exists in my realm. His current goal would change that. He wants our worlds to merge. He has declared war on reality and wants to use me to combine the worlds."

This is crazy. This is so much worse than I realized. I remain silent for a moment before finally asking, "What am I supposed to do about it? Is there a way for you to come to my world and sever the connection in order to trap him here?"

She slowly shakes her head and says, "I want nothing more than to exist as a normal person in your world, but the man believes if the embodiment of this world that you see before you now were to enter reality, the worlds would merge, allowing him to maintain his power. I would likely destroy reality by existing in it."

She begins to tear up again and continues, "I spent centuries trying to emulate a world like yours, but I have lost control, and it's all gone and turned to waste."

"I'm still not seeing how I can help in all this," I reply.

"I will teach you!" she says. "You can master this reality just like that man. You have an advantage, as you have a teacher. He taught me far more than I was ever able to teach him. Your first task is to learn how to control your surroundings."

Chapter 25

Controlling your surroundings seems pretty advanced for something to begin with. I wish the first lesson would be to learn how to leave this place.

"How am I going to jump right into controlling my surroundings when I have no basic knowledge on how to do anything in this world?" I ask.

"Don't you realize?" she says. "You have been influencing this world from the moment you came here. You have a natural talent that far exceeds almost anyone else who has arrived here. I see so much potential."

"What are you talking about?" I respond.

"Do you not remember the first time you came here?" she asks.

"Yes. I remember too much. It was a nightmare—" I begin.

"No," she interrupts. "It was no nightmare. It was as real as your mind made it. You created all that you saw. From the moment you first entered this world, your mind has melded with it. This is how you control your surroundings. This is how that man controls his surroundings."

I don't know if I can believe all this. It kind of makes sense. Wait. No, it doesn't. But when has anything here made sense? I created my own nightmare when I believed I was in the real world. What else did I create? I look down at myself and the belongings I have carried with me. My bag, the binoculars, maybe even the quick exit from the man's study. Did I make it all happen?

I finally ask, "How? How is this all possible?"

She immediately winces in sadness. "These accomplishments of yours are skills. These have come to you naturally. All you have to do is use your mind and believe. The possibilities are endless."

"Like a dream," I say. "When I dream lucidly, it can still be difficult to control the dream and even to stay asleep."

"This is not a dream you can wake up from," she says.

"Unless I go back to the real world. Why did you think sending me back like that would be helpful?" I ask.

"I never said that I sent you back. I said I wanted to. You went back on your own before I could say any more." She smiles and says, "You're a natural."

My heart sinks at the realization. All the implications. I am overwhelmed. She acts like this isn't strange. I feel light and stumble back. The smile she's giving me turns to a look of deep concern as she watches me fall back. Everything is slow. The concern turns to horror. I see her eyes go dark and burst with tears as she appears to lose control of her face. Like a frightened child. The rest of her face turns dark. No, everything is going dark. I jolt my body out of fading consciousness. I look forward. Everything's still dark. Everything is silent.

Part 4

Chapter 26

"What's happening?" I ask, hoping for a response.

Nothing.

I can tell that I'm still standing upright. I thought I fell, but somehow, I'm still on my feet. The air feels cold. It's alarming to me, as I haven't felt cold in a long while. I feel noticeably different. Although I feel where I am, I still cannot see or hear anything at all. I try to take a step forward but slam my face into a wall. I can definitely tell that I'm still in a cave. I have no choice but to hug the wall and try to find my way. No use in standing still.

As I keep the wall within my reach, I finally arrive to an area of the cave that is letting in a faint light. The light gets brighter and brighter as I approach. The cave opens up and reveals many machines of which I cannot tell the function. They are near, and many even connect to a strange, decrepit metal tube that seems to have once been used by people, as there is a door on the side. The light source seems to be coming from the machines and door. I walk into the tube past the door and find another door. It seems that I'm in a room that functions similar to an airlock. Not sure what the purpose actually is. There is another door that leads inside. It's locked with a keypad.

At this point, I don't care what happens next. I'm fed up. I decide to knock on the door as loudly as I can. So what if I run into another lunatic? But, of course, there is no response. It honestly doesn't even look like the keypad would work. I finally give the door a good kick. I feel it give a bit. It doesn't seem to actually be locked. I can see through a crack in the door that there are a large number of objects stacked behind it. Chairs and tables. I start ramming the door, and little by little, it opens. The corridor I have now entered is dimly lit, as most of the lights are out. It's dank and dirty in here. Despite that, it appears similar to a military setup. There's equipment and architecture I've seen before, though incomplete. For all I know, assets are being pulled from my mind as if my brain is a database for a video game. It's like going someplace the developers don't want you to see yet. I can't help to think I might be a pawn in some game in one way or another. Regardless, I continue onward. This corridor doesn't seem to be completed as I pass unfinished side rooms hooking off from the main corridor. I approach an elevator at the end of the corridor and press the button to see if it works. To my surprise, the doors open with a squeal. I walk in and look at my options. There is only one other floor. I press the button, and the elevator goes up. Strangely, the elevator seems to be working just fine.

The doors open and reveal a gate on the inside of a complex. It looks highly secured. The floor looks like it's still in use, and I think I hear some movement on the other side of the gate.

"Is anybody there!" I yell.

Someone opens the gate and gazes at me. He asks, "How did you get back there? Are you trying to pull a trick?"

Is this for real? Am I actually back? Or is my mind creating fake scenarios? It feels so real. The hope builds up in my mind, and a spastic smile uncontrollably stretches across my face. This is real?

The soldier who questioned me is suspicious, and my smile likely only makes him more skeptical, but I can't help it.

I decide to be honest and say, "I came from the elevator."

"Yeah, right," he says. "That elevator hasn't been used in years. As you should be aware, we do not tolerate pranks, especially concerning that elevator."

He calls over his buddy, and they detain me and take all of my possessions. They put me in a holding cell, which, at a closer glance, seems closer to a kennel. It's a small room carved into a rock wall appropriated into a cage.

After waiting a couple hours, they tell me the chief will be down to talk with me. Soon thereafter, I hear footsteps approach my cell. The chief turns to look into my dark cell. It's a familiar face. It looks like the same guy I worked under before I got trapped in the other world. But he looks worse for wear. I approach the door and say, "It's great to see you! I could use a debriefing for what the heck is going…"

The chief faints.

Chapter 27

A couple of soldiers standing with the chief catch him before he hits the ground. The chief quickly comes to.

Still embraced by the soldiers, he looks at me in a confused manner and asks, "How?"

Equally as confused, I respond by saying, "The elevator."

The chief, now back on his feet, raises his voice and shouts, "After ten long years!"

My eyes bulge out of my head at the thought. Does he look like this because he's older?

"Ten years?" I repeat nervously. My heart sinks at the thought. No, I have to be skeptical. It doesn't make sense. He must be exaggerating.

"Follow me to my office," he commands. "I'm contacting the general about this. I'm sure he's going to want to see you."

"General?" I repeat. Why would a general want to see me?

I walk with him back to his office. The noticeably more spacious room shows things appear a bit more high-tech due to the compactness of the technology, but he's maintained his office to look like the one I remember. Maybe the tech advancement is in my head.

He walks around his desk and sits in his chair. He picks up his phone and presses one button. I hear someone on the other end immediately. "Get me the general!" he demands. He pauses for a moment, looks back at me, and says, "Someone's come back."

Chapter 28

Within the hour, a general comes marching through the door. It is no one I recognize. Regardless, it is very surprising that he was so close by that he could just come here personally. After halting before us, he closes the door and calmly asks, "What do you know about the other side?"

I take my time in responding. I don't know what to say. I ask, "What do you want to know about this…'other side'?"

Frustrated by my answer, the general responds, "Anyone that goes missing is never found. Anyone that goes searching for the lost are themselves never found. All we do find in these no-go zones are feral, demented creatures that attack anything they see, even each other. They are the only living things that have no trouble traversing these zones. You are the first person to ever be lost and make it back. Strangely, from the pictures I've seen, it appears that after ten years gone, you look better than when you left. Why is that?"

"Listen, it doesn't feel like it's been ten years," I begin. "Maybe several weeks at most. It's honestly hard to tell. How do I know all this time has actually passed, other than the chief looking worse for wear here? I don't trust any of this enough to be giving you answers that you may be looking for."

He gives me a look of shock as if he didn't realize I don't yet believe the chief's claim. With a puzzled face, he asks, "You serious?" Then, he shakes his head and waves his hand at me as he says, "It doesn't matter. I'm bringing you to the board and you can give answers on the record." He then points at me and says, "Even if you don't think time has passed since your disappearance, a lot has changed. You'll come to realize this soon enough."

He gestures for me to get up from my seat and follow him out of the office. As I follow, two MPs trail us. As we get outside, something jolts my subconscious. I feel startled and I'm not sure why. The outside is cool, and the sky is overcast. Looking into the sky, the realization kicks in. The sky is a hue of purple that is reminiscent of the world I thought I left behind. The time of day seems to be in the twilight hours.

The general notices my pause. "Is something the matter?" he asks with a smirk. He notices my eyes locked on to the sky and says, "The sky has looked the same for years. Unchanging. Can't see the sun. Can't tell night from day. There is no moon or stars. Telecommunications have begun to fail. We have no connection to our satellites. Heh, if we fly too high, our electronics malfunction. We can't even make it across the ocean anymore. We are cut off... A lot has happened."

The escort finally arrives at a helicopter parked outside the base. We all hop in and take off. As we rise, I get to see the city skyline and what is clearly San Francisco from the presence of the Golden Gate Bridge. The bay itself, though, looks completely different, as if the bridge was transplanted over to another city. Then, looking at the city itself, it is littered with garbage, and buildings are a mess. There is so much damage to the streets; it looks as if there has been no upkeep in quite some time. Still, people walk the streets. Stores and lights are viewable, but the city looks like all the worst parts of Detroit. The most shocking of all is the wall that now surrounds much of the city. I can see it in the distance, encircling the outskirts of the city region. As I get a glimpse of beyond the wall, there is nothing. It is barren. Trees are barely present.

"What happened?" I ask.

"Chaos," the general responds. "Like I said, things have changed. We don't know why. We know the origins of the turmoil are those darn no-go zones. We hope you can shed some light on the issues before society finally reaches that point of no return and crumbles."

Chapter 29

After a brief flight, I arrive at a board room of high-ranking government officials. I am gestured to take a seat at one end of the table. I sit and wait patiently to be spoken to. There is a long pause as people are still prepping for the meeting. There are people seated around the edge of the room as well as the large table. I feel like a diplomat having just arrived at a third world country. I can tell things don't work the same as they used to.

The general sits at the other end of the table and addresses me. "First, you have not been fully briefed. A lot has changed since you went MIA. San Francisco has become one of the nation's largest strongholds. Most of the other large strongholds are coastal, either bordering ocean or lakes. Travel between strongholds on the West Coast to the strongholds of the Great Lakes is incredibly dangerous. The outer lands are hostile not just from the monsters crawling out of cracks in the earth, but also from a lack of authority. Travel across the country has created Oregon Trail-type scenarios. There are no rural areas anymore, at least not in the traditional sense. The urban areas are in the process of falling apart. The country's population is under one hundred million for the first time since the beginning of the twentieth century. We foresee the collapse of society nearing every day. The world is crumbling around it, and we want to stop it."

This last statement has caused people to stir in their seats. He pauses for a brief moment before continuing, "I brought you here because you have been to the source of the devastation and returned. The only known person to do so.

Three of your belongings we confiscated were found to be peculiar after a close analysis. These items were of unknown material origin. In fact, their compositions make no sense. It's impossible to tell how they were manufactured or how they even exist in the first place. It's like some kind of quantum effect could be causing this, but that is a proposed idea I lack the understanding to explain, and I don't believe having it explained would be helpful. I think that because I heard the explanation and still don't get it. But from what the scientists have conveyed, they can't quite understand it either. I have brought the items with me."

He proceeds to place each one on the table. It's a pair of binoculars, the man's notebook, and his locked journal. But the lock has been broken! "The binoculars are hardly functional. The journal took some time to break open, but all the pages are blank. The one item of interest we found is this lab notebook. Where did you find these items?" he asks, staring at me intently.

This is a lot to take in all at once. The guy hardly takes a breath. He's treating this so casually. It takes me a minute to process everything that was said and what is being asked.

"Well?" someone seated at the table spouts out in a frustrated manner.

I sigh. "I assume you've seen the contents of the notebook then?"

The general, unblinking, makes strong eye contact with me. With his unwavering stare, he says, "Yes, we have. We need to know where you got this."

So, I tell them about the manor on the farm. I tell them about the man. I tell them about the shapeshifting woman claiming to be a god. I tell them about the woman I found hanging, waiting to be another of the man's experiments. I tell them about the study. I tell them all that I can remember.

Of course, my accounts of the "other world" are met with healthy skepticism. Reality is crumbling around them, and most of them find my story too farfetched. The general doesn't. He proceeds with the inquiry despite calls to end the meeting, as some people see it as a waste of time. The general asks me about the binoculars, as I didn't mention them.

I begin, "I tried to use them for recon. As I observed the manor from the outside, I noticed I had binoculars on me. I don't really know where they came from. They didn't even work. They only started to work, very poorly, when I no longer needed them."

"Why was that?" the general asks.

I haven't had much time to process anything. Everything that's happened since I left the other world has occurred nonstop. I haven't had much time to reflect back on all that I've gone through. According to the general, the last good night of sleep I had was over ten years ago. Regardless, I comply with a legitimate answer that unfortunately matches my crippled state of mind.

"I made those binoculars," I say. "They didn't work until I put my mind on getting them to work. In that world, it's all about our minds. Our consciousness. What we will to be, will be… in the world the man calls 'unreality.' I escaped from the crazed madman by creating a literal escape hatch under his desk in the study. It's taken me a while to believe it, but it's the only explanation."

I didn't realize but as I spoke, I started to talk faster and louder. I sound crazier and crazier, judging by the feel in the room. I think some of the people in the room feel threatened by the looks they're giving. Everyone is wide-eyed and staring at me as they sink deeper into their seats. After an awkward pause, I am approached by soldiers, and I assume I am about to get kicked out. I need to be taken seriously, but could anyone take what I just said seriously? I see someone look down at their lap and shake their head as if embarrassed to be in the room.

Trying to explain myself better, I say, "Listen, we have literal rips in reality connecting to another world. If you all even half believe that, please hear me out and don't disregard what I have to say."

The general raises his hand in a stop motion as a gesture for the soldiers approaching me to halt. "Please continue," he says. "Just try to stay calm."

I take a large inhale and slowly breathe out. My blood pressure is through the roof. I can feel the blood coursing through my veins. I must be red in the face.

"I know all this because of the deity of that world, or the world itself being the deity who lacks control of itself. It has a personified form containing its consciousness. The form reached out to me for help. The man is actually more of a god in that world than she is, and he's human."

"Hold on. She?" someone interjects.

Part of me is surprised that someone in this room is actually following any of this. "She chose her form to be that of mother earth since she admires this world so much," I respond. "Maybe you can go back to the hole you climbed out of and tell her to leave us alone," they respond in a sarcastic tone.

"She has no control," I say. "I already told you, that madman has more control than she does."

"So, she asked for help," says the general. "How could you possibly help her?"

I look down at the table and say, "By becoming as powerful as that man. Becoming a god of that world. She believes the human mind has greater potential than hers in doing so. Unfortunately, the world will mess with your mind, or more accurately, your mind will mess with you. My first experiences there were like dreams, but dreams that have come to life. It can be too difficult to discern the dream from reality. It can be even harder to get a grip on how the world is shaped around you. Apparently, it took me years."

There's a long silence. No one seems to want to entertain me any longer.

"Any more questions?" asks the general.

One person packs their things and says, "I think we're done here." Others follow suit.

"I guess the meeting is over," the general says as he walks over to me. He then bends down to me and says in a muffled voice, "I believe you. I've seen more things I can't explain than an average man would see in ten lifetimes. I think it's time to start believing. I have a room for you at a hotel down the street. Free room service. Get some rest and stick around. You can hold on to the journal and binoculars. I don't have interest in those. I'm going to hold on to the lab notebook, though." He pats me on the back and walks off.

Chapter 30

I make my way straight to the hotel. I am shown my room and collapse upon the bed. As I lie there, my mind swirls with thought. I think back to my walk over here. It was bizarre walking through the streets I once knew. They were much more crowded. The air is also stale.

I stare at the ceiling and feel overcome with exhaustion. I allow my consciousness to fade.

My body is weightless, and I feel comfortable, almost happy. Suddenly, I hear a loud bang at the door. I try to ignore it and hope whoever it is will go away. I hear another loud bang on the door. Then another. It's getting louder and more aggressive. I angrily sit up and shout, "What!" What I hear next inflicts pain throughout my body. It's the voice of the man.

"It's time. I have something special for you," he says in a mischievous voice.

Panicked, I quickly look around for an escape. As I search, I realize I'm not in the hotel room. I'm back in that room. That bedroom at his manor he trapped me in before.

He gently opens the door to reveal his smiling face. He then says, "I've been eagerly preparing this just for you!" With a small gesture of his hand, he makes the room shift around us as if we are falling through the floor into the depths of his dungeon. I feel my stomach lift into my throat.

I can't move my arms. I look up to see my hands impaled through a meat hook attached to the ceiling. He slowly walks up to me and pinches the skin on my torso. His smile grows unnaturally wide as it approaches my face. He looks deep into my eyes and begins peeling off the skin he's grabbing. I want to scream, but nothing comes out. I'm now fully immobile. He takes a large cleaver. I feel completely helpless, as I know he is about to butcher me alive. He starts at my thigh and digs into my flesh. As he hits the femoral artery, blood comes rushing out and pools beneath his feet. I want nothing more than to pass out and stop the suffering, but I stay conscious. As he pulls the flesh from my bone, he digs into my hip and pops out the joint. I did not know the human body was capable of feeling this much pain. His stare persists, and his smile does not fade. My blood has been pulsating out of my wound and has covered the both of us. His smile is now bloodied. He tilts his head and his smile finally fades into a serious look. His stare singes my soul. He lifts a smaller knife and moves it toward my eye. I try not to look, but my eyes will not close. I see him methodically begin to cut into my eye, and everything begins to grow dark.

I finally manage to belch out a loud scream. I open my eyes to see I am still in the hotel room. I look at the clock. I've hardly slept an hour. And to think I was looking forward to sleep.

Chapter 31

Days have passed. I haven't left my hotel room. I haven't heard a word from anybody. I've spent my days feasting on deliveries from room service and watching old movies. There is no internet or cable. I don't know if those are commonplace anymore. They're likely too broken to give people access. The hotel has notified me that only one week of my stay has been paid for and that week is almost up. I have no choice but to head out and see if there is anything more I can do at base. There has to be more.

I gather up the motivation to head outside. As I enter this dark world of reality once again, I notice it is quite a bit colder than I remember San Francisco typically getting. I can see my breath. The people I pass look dreary. There is an overwhelming sense of hopelessness. Most of the people in these crowds appear to be homeless. I know this city had a reputation for its homeless population, but this is absurd.

As I get to the base, I am greeted by armed guards at the gate. I ask to speak to the chief, but they turn me away. They admit to me that they have orders to bar my entry. The top heads must find me unreliable. They probably didn't like seeing high-ranking military personnel entertain my words after hearing how crazy it all sounds. They probably believe I'm polluting their minds. I can't blame them too much. But I find issue that I can't even do grunt work. I've got no direction outside the military, and from what it looks like around here, there's not much I can be doing.

As I turn the corner around the block headed back to my hotel, a woman walks up to me and says, "I was waiting for you."

I recognize her from that meeting that went south. She was silent in that room.

She then says, "Despite the helpful notebook, they don't trust you…but they have been watching. They've even had eyes in your hotel room. I'm assigned to watch you whenever you leave and was waiting for you, but I didn't expect you to be such a hermit. Now that I've got your attention, I'll have you know that they don't see you at the moment, as I'm their eyes right now. I'm not even supposed to interact with you."

"Why are you telling me this?" I ask.

"Because I believe you," she responds. "I want to help fix our world, and I believe you are the key."

"That's weird. The general seemed to believe me and yet he hasn't reached out," I say skeptically.

"He's a loyal dog," she explains. "He does what he's told whether he agrees with it or not. He won't help you. I can. I know how to get you back to the other world. There are others that want to help."

I give myself a moment to respond. After deciding, I sigh and say, "I'm sorry, lady. Being cut loose has put a thought in my mind. I need to see my family."

"Your family is on the other side of the country. You'll never make it to them," she responds.

Her words click in my mind. I grab her and demand, "Tell me what you know about my family."

"Less than you'd like," she says. "I just know where you're from and where they were."

I let go of her and say, "I'm leaving today." I feel my heart pulling me towards those I love. I can use the travel time to reflect on everything that has transpired. I'm not eager to jump back into the insanity of the other world.

"You're leaving to see a family that may already be gone?" she asks. "Most of the country is gone, consumed by the corruption of this world or from their own doing. You have no idea—"

"I don't care," I interrupt. I need to know how they are. I need to see them. I don't know if I'll get the opportunity again when I finally find the resolve to face the plague upon our world.

She's clearly not happy and must find me unreasonable, but she says desperately, "I'll help you get there as long as you go back to this…unreality and end what I believe to be the apocalypse. I know it might be a long shot, but from what horrors I have seen from top secret briefings, we have to take the chance."

"Listen," I respond. "It's nice of you to offer your help, but if I ever do go back to that miserable existence in the other world, no one else is coming with me. If that lunatic from the other world doesn't get them, their own minds certainly will. Your mind can consume you in that place. I don't know if it was luck or something else entirely, but I had the best-case scenario where I regained control of my mental state. However, from what it looks like, it took me ten years. No other soul is known to have done the same. I don't think now is the time for people to start trying. So, if you're going to help, do it fast because I'm not sticking around."

"I need to come with you," she says firmly. "I know the safest way to the East Coast. I know the strongholds and places to avoid. We'd have to hit Salt Lake, get to the Great Lakes, and then we can get to Boston from Buffalo. If your family is still around, they'd probably still be near Boston. Some places along the coast we have to avoid, like Philly and New York City. That whole region is lit up in chaos. Baltimore and D.C. are also gone. The government decentralized, and these cities strayed too far and consumed themselves."

She keeps talking, but I stop listening. I start to walk away and say, "Thanks for the valuable information. I'll keep it in mind."

She runs in front of me and says, "I can get us supplies. AR-15s, 9mm pistols, plenty of ammunition, food, and water, as well as provide methods of transportation. It's a tough environment out there. The trips are going to be long, so I'll get us some reliable vehicles. I know stops on the way where we can restock. Money is not an issue." She pauses for a moment and looks down in realization. "Once we get to Buffalo, we'll need bikes. The terrain has shifted, and large vehicles aren't practical past a certain point."

"You seem excited. All I have heard is how dangerous it is," I say.

"I'm full of mixed emotions. I always wanted to travel the country, admittedly before the end of the world began, but I still haven't been able to go to any of these areas. I have the knowledge needed to do this. The danger doesn't scare me. Especially if I'm with you. I know all about you. I think I'll be quite safe. And you can count on me to watch your back," she says with a smile. "Besides, I want to make sure this world gets saved. So many people have lost hope. I haven't. This world is worth saving."

Chapter 32

I take a final bite of my breakfast before I get booted from the hotel. Despite the apocalyptic nature of society, this hotel seems to still be able to make spectacular dishes. They clearly have access to foods most people can't get their hands on. I can understand why the military is only paying for a one-week stay. I can't imagine how costly this must be.

I look out my window and wait for the signal. She told me she would attach a garment with hearts on it to a clothesline that I can see from my hotel window. I see it. Somehow, I think what is supposed to be inconspicuous is incredibly conspicuous. I see an enormous old-fashioned pair of women's undergarments speckled with large hearts like straight out of a cartoon. I cannot fathom where she got her hands on those. At least people are still capable of such humor in dark times.

The signal means to head to our rendezvous point. It's a hall, which is a large building long since abandoned even before I ever went to that other world. It's quite a walk away, technically outside of the city but still within urban protected limits.

On the walk, I don't see the thriving American city I remember. It much more closely resembles the third world. The roads haven't been paved in years and contain more dirt than asphalt. Street markets are all over. Few cars are in the crumbling roads. This city has not been maintained. Sewage systems don't seem very efficient as I pass some areas where it has pooled. There's sewage spilling into streets from apartments buildings. The stink is horrible.

I see a vendor selling old cassettes, CDs and vinyl records. They've got some great hits. I hope we'll be traveling in an older car with a disc player because I'm definitely grabbing what I can. Most online media is hardly functional with the way of the world and I'd rather depend on the old stuff. Looking at what else there is to offer around this area, I don't see much of interest. Most of the other vendors are just selling old junk and sketchy food. I proceed to my destination without many more distractions.

Once I arrive at the hall, I see the area has been repurposed into a street skating area. A bunch of teenagers are doing their best to skateboard. I may not skate, but I can see they're novices struggling to even do shuvits. They've got no pop.

As I'm enamored by the teens, someone yells, "Hey!" and grabs my shoulder from behind. I get startled and turn around, reflexively pushing them back and almost knocking them down.

As soon as she regains her balance, she exclaims, "Wow! Sorry, I didn't mean to surprise you!" She breathes out to calm herself, as she was startled by my response. "Come on. The goods are this way." She gestures to the direction she came from with a wave of her arm.

We approach two black SUVs. She opens the trunks and reveals the arms and other supplies. She hands me a walkie-talkie, closes the trunks, hands me a set of keys, and then says, "Utah is our first stop. It won't be too hard to get to. Just follow me and do as I say."

We get into our own separate vehicles and head to the urban protected limits. The gate we approach has armed guards. She gets to the gate first and appears to hand them identification. They walk away to their windowed security room. She then speaks into the walkie-talkie. "Your government ID is in the glove compartment." I open the glove compartment to find an official government ID. It's up to date. I honestly never even thought about this. She then further explains, "That is indeed your actual newly issued government identification badge. That can be used anywhere in the country. Hand it to the guards and we'll be on our way. The government officials don't want you leaving, but the guards won't know. The people that do know won't care enough to follow after you. Sorry to say, but you aren't exactly a high priority to keep."

I show my ID to the guards, and we head out into the outer lands.

Chapter 33

The journey to Salt Lake is long and uneventful. Gas stations are rare commodities, often in urban areas, which we need to avoid. I'm told it's like Mad Max out there. There's no real law enforcement, and there are few people to govern. Anarchy reigns in most of the country. We make sure to stay in the more rural areas. Rural areas have almost nobody, as they are very dangerous. The previous lack of people and invasion of otherworldly creatures causes a dangerous situation where there are few people who can help.

She tells me that the monsters in these areas aren't the ones I've seen. These areas contain demented chimeras. Mangled combinations of animals. Despite her suggestion of the infestation of animal amalgamations, these areas seem mostly lifeless. There's nothing. Hardly any vegetation. What remains looks sickly. I can't tell if it's being resilient or if it's being smothered out of existence. There's hardly any movement to be seen. Such silence. I left an environment where I was witnessing the fading of humanity, but I think I'm witnessing the fading of life itself.

We've only just passed Sacramento. There was no hassle. The main threat of the area is hijackers stealing vehicles. Sacramento is completely anarchic. No law enforcement or medical care. We've also got a lot of gasoline, as we can't risk a stop, which makes our situation more dangerous. Thankfully, no one ever came in sight. I have mixed feelings about traveling so far without seeing a single living soul. I'm admittedly thankful I'm not alone. I've spent a lot of time alone, and it's nice to finally have consistent contact with another human being.

The drive seems like it can only get easier as we approach Nevada and there is mostly desert ahead. Yet, she stops the car, and I halt behind her. She speaks in a calm, soft tone through the walkie-talkie, but with a sense of urgency. "Turn off your car." I do just as she asks. Then, I see it.

There's what looks like a black bear with the head of a bobcat. It also has oversized antlers. It has some small creature in its mouth. It looks like it could also be some amalgamation, but it's hard to tell, as it's completely mangled. The smaller creature doesn't appear to be dead, though. It's twitching. Could be post-mortem twitches. I really don't know. It doesn't acknowledge our vehicles. As I stare at it, I can't help but to chuckle at the first sign of a threat. It's a grotesque beast, but its movements are awkward, and it seems to barely be able to hold up its antlers due to their enormous size. Its head doesn't fit its body. I know exactly who is responsible for its creation, and I think less of him now.

I pick up the walkie-talkie and whisper, "Look at that thing's head. It's so small. The body's so fat. It can barely lift its head with those doofy antlers. I don't know what that guy was thinking. More proof he's lost his mind." I honestly have trouble getting the words out without making too much noise from laughter. As disgusting of a creature this is, its existence is hilarious. Almost adorable. Maybe I've also gone and lost my mind. I hear her try to respond, but she's struggling to contain a laugh. She went from legitimately scared to laughing at danger. As soon as the circus animal moves out of sight, we stop holding back and burst into laughter. Laughter is contagious, and we feed off each other in a seemingly endless cycle. We go on our merry way. I feel I've gone mad.

"I almost want to see more of these weird creations. That was quite the sight to behold," I tell her.

"Who's *that guy* you were referring to?" she asks.

"You don't know what's in the lab book I brought back?" I ask. "The crazy dude did experiments. One was on a bear. Definitely wasn't the one we saw."

"No, I know about that," she says. "The way you put it just didn't click in my mind. We're not likely to see much else before Salt Lake. Go listen to your Led Zeppelin to avoid getting too bored."

"You noticed? I can lend you some classics if you'd like or at least provide you with some great recommendations. Oh, and, uh, you'll definitely be hearing from me if I get too bored," I say.

Chapter 34

We manage to get to Salt Lake City after one night of rest. Like San Francisco, the city region is walled off. We use our government-issued IDs and get in no problem. This city is a breath of fresh air compared to San Francisco. Dry air, admittedly. Not as much area is contained, but what is being protected is much more well kept. It still looks like an urban area and not falling apart. This place seems to have a comparable population to San Francisco, but people look a lot more content here…for the most part. The apocalypse has stayed outside their walls.

Despite this city's people giving me a greater sense of hope, we don't stay long. We treat this as a pit stop to resupply. The trip to the Great Lakes will be even longer and possibly much more eventful. Chicago is the next stop.

When grabbing snacks and fuel, I couldn't help but to say to the shop clerk, "I just came from the west coast. Over there, it looks like the world's end is right around the corner. This place is a far cry from that. Know anything about Chicago?"

"That whole region around the Great Lakes is relatively unchanged just like right here." They respond. "Quite a trip you're making. Not too many people would be willing to do something like that these days."

"Admittedly, I'm not like too many people," I say. "Have a good day."

Hearing this news, I gain comfort knowing we should be able to safely travel between Chicago and Buffalo with minimal issues. Unfortunately, getting to that point won't necessarily be easy. Hopefully nothing goes wrong. There isn't a whole lot to be threatened by in the Midwest, as much of it has always been fairly empty.

I grab more CDs for entertainment. This time audio books and comedy specials.

Back to the open road. They say it only gets bumpier.

Chapter 35

We pass through Wyoming with no trouble. There were no monster sightings, or anything else really. Surprisingly, there was on occasion a self-sufficient town relatively untouched by the deterioration of the world. Never saw anything hostile. These settlements left over from the times before show humanity's ability to adapt and persevere. It's quite admirable. We'd even pass other vehicles on the road from time to time. That's something we never saw in California and was still rare once we left the state. This is all despite far fewer people living in these barren areas. If I had crawled out of a cave in Wyoming, I might've taken quite a bit longer to realize anything was wrong. It comes as a shock to her. She somehow didn't know there were so many places better off than the city where she's been confined. She supposedly has so much knowledge on the state of the nation and the routes forward, but I can tell she's losing confidence in her perception of her home. The blindfold has been lifted, and all the doom and gloom aren't all they seem to be. The circumstances are dire, but we shouldn't lose faith in humanity.

As we pass Lincoln, Nebraska, we take an unexpected pit stop. We were planning to continue on until Chicago, but it seems there are more strongholds than she knew about. Lincoln has law enforcement. First responders are here and active.

We make our stop at a large grocery store to grab snacks, stretch our legs, and rest for a while. She's not going into the store, though. She has gotten out of her vehicle and hasn't moved. I approach and see that she's awestruck by her surroundings.

"Are you all right?" I ask.

"I haven't seen people living life like this since I was a kid. To see an actual supermarket not repurposed into a shelter..." She pauses and breathes deeply as if getting lightheaded and overwhelmed. She then says, "Most people struggle to get the money for food and resort to trade and stealing. There are government rations, but people still go to bed hungry. Where I'm from, only the wealthy or well-connected live well. I was lucky enough to have a soft non-infested bed to sleep in."

"Well," I begin. "Groveling isn't going to fill our bellies. Let's take a look at what they've got inside."

We enter the store and see a good number of people shopping casually. The shelves aren't very full, but they're also far from empty. Admittedly, the majority of the food in here is in the produce and butcher areas. As we look through, she wanders off. She can hardly stand still and is running around, looking at everything this place has to offer like a kid in a candy store. I feel like I'd need a leash to not lose her.

She comes up to me with loads of veggies and fruits in hand and says, "Why can't San Francisco be like this? There are tons of farms around."

"There are a whole bunch of factors," I respond. "There's population difference, location, and even how it's governed. I can tell you self-sufficiency is very important. If you're relying on the government all the time, you're not going to do well in the apocalypse. You could get away with poor governance under normal circumstances...as long as it doesn't get worse too fast. The world going down in flames is a stress test your city didn't handle too well. At least they survived. That should count for something." I chuckle and continue, "You know, ten years ago, different people, the news, politicians…they all made the world seem so grim. They know now what grim really is."

She's not very happy with my response and approaches an employee stocking the produce. I may have upset her. She asks them where they get their food in a demanding tone. I hear the man say, "There are farms everywhere. The strangeness of these times has lowered their production, but they still keep up." "I'm not from around here," she says. "Could you elaborate?"

"Well, the sky doesn't act ideal for crops anymore, but the farms still produce," he says. "Thankfully, we haven't had so much of the troubles I've been hearing about across the country. Stories of monsters. I have heard of sightings around here and some people's experiences, but I've never seen one myself. Well, that's not completely true. I should say I haven't seen any in a long time. A few years back, we had a large influx of these gross creatures. Awful times, I tell you. But that's in the past now. We handled it well, and they are rare sightings now. We've got people who can handle them when they do pop up."

"Can you tell me of that time…a few years back?" she asks.

"Listen," started the man. "We lost a lot of folks. Those creatures were hopping out of the ground, popping into people's homes." He pauses for a moment. He's clearly having trouble talking about it.

"Please! Continue. I really need to know," she says as she keeps pushing for more with her bright and wide glowing eyes.

"Police were overwhelmed. What little military we had around couldn't compensate. Hospitals overflowed with injured and dead. It took normal people to rise up and stomp out the diseased monsters. We had to protect ourselves and then help those around us. It was a terrible time, and I'm proud of what we accomplished."

She's stunned by this guy's story. Her eyes have grown dark. After an awkward silence, she says, "I'm sorry. That's awful." She's not so riled up anymore. "At least your local area has things figured out."

"Not really," he responds. "The monsters may be much less of a threat, but the sky is still in ceaseless twilight. Nothing but a faint glow of sunlight to feed the crops. Farmers have resorted to using tall lamps out in the field during the day to get crops extra light. It's just not practical to keep working, especially when things have only been getting worse. The air is getting colder. The crop yield is slowly waning. Outside the farms, a lot is dying. I really don't know how long we'll be able to go on living like normal. People are getting scared. The people you see around you don't lose hope, but I can tell it's starting to fade away."

She's now anxiously looking at her feet, unwilling to look at the guy's clearly upset face. Then she says, "I really appreciate the talk. I should be going. Things will get better soon. I know it. Please…have a nice day."

She walks back over to me and tugs my arm. As she pulls me away, she says, "We need to get going. We shouldn't be making any unnecessary pit stops. I want to be in Chicago as soon as possible."

That's not something I could fathom many people saying. Regardless, we pick up a few things, hop in our cars, and head straight for Chicago.

Chapter 36

Chicago comes much quicker than Salt Lake. My mind has been very occupied. Part of me doesn't want the drive to end because I just don't want to move on. Yet, I'm already here. The travel only gets easier until Buffalo. Chicago is very noisy. There are many people here, and sirens from emergency vehicles are constantly blasting down streets. I can't tell if the city is under so much stress from the world circumstances or if it's Chicago being Chicago.

Somehow, the first major sign of danger we run into is inside the city. Crossing the outskirts of the city at night, a truck drives in front of us and blocks the road. Looking behind us, there is another truck blocking an escape. Men get out of the cars and surround us. They brandish their weapons and show clear hostility. Pointing shotguns at our cars, a couple of them start to yell at us to get out of our cars.

She gets out of her car slowly with her hands on her head, and a couple of them hop in the car. I take my time to respond.

It's not been more than ten seconds of screaming, and the men seem increasingly agitated. Three men are on my driver side, threatening to shoot if I didn't do what they say. One man is standing right on the other side of the window with his gun pointing one inch away from the window. So, I slowly open the door as they want. The dimwit standing inches from me as I get out seems to be far too confident. They don't even have their fingers on their triggers. They weren't planning to shoot. Maybe they are desperate. Maybe they like taking advantage of the weak.

I push the guy's gun away from my direction and quickly slug him in the face. I immediately pull my concealed handgun out from under my coat and firmly place it under his chin. He immediately drops his weapon and gives me a look of terror. I look behind him, and all I see are the two who were standing with him now running away as fast as they can. As soon as the other guys get a whiff of what's going down, they take off. I let the guy go but maintain gunpoint until he's out of sight.

After all is said and done, now utterly terrified, she puts her hands down and says, "That was…I don't know what to say. Thank you. That was amazing. We would've lost everything if you didn't do that."

"Instead, we lost half of everything," I replied.

Her stunned, relieved expression fades as quickly as it appeared.

"We need to trade in the car for a rust bucket. Our cars were too conspicuous," I say. "Hop in." I open the passenger car door for her, and she gets in. As I'm about to close the door, I stop myself and ask, "You like Zeppelin?"

She doesn't respond and remains expressionless. I can't help but to smile as I get in, then turn on my tunes.

Chapter 37

Despite losing half of all of our supplies, we make it to Buffalo without running out. Not many pit stops were needed. After getting robbed, we thought we should stop only sparingly.

I have questioned her choice in direction as there may have been a better path, but she frequently answers without saying anything. Words come out, but have no meaning. She dodges my interrogations. But finally, she has begun to open up and has admitted to me that she chose this route not necessarily because it was the safest, but because her family is from here. She's never been to the place so much of her family has resided and wanted the opportunity to meet them. After my request to see my family, I can't say I'm upset.

We arrive at a hotel and settle in for a while. I let her know I don't mind if she goes out to see her family for the day and we can set back out tomorrow. She gives little pause and heads out. It leaves me on my own to ponder.

I could go out and check out the town, see how the people are making it through these trying times, but my mind can't help but to go to the nightmares. Restful sleep is not something I've had. The first sleep I had back in the real world was just the beginning of a pattern. I haven't wanted to confront my fears, but I know I have to. I have to if I ever want to succeed. It's a long shot, and I don't feel like I will make it with my mind intact, or even my life. I just don't have a choice. It's either try or give up. Giving up will have the same result, not just for me but for everyone. But if I fail, my time would just come sooner, and everyone else will still suffer the same fate.

I'm having trouble getting my mind around what I should do. I have had thoughts to just end it. The pressure is too great. It all seems so hopeless. It's such a terrible mindset. I turned myself into a warrior to defend life no matter the cost. I can't give in. It doesn't matter if the odds are a trillion to one. I know I have to try. I will face my inner demons, acknowledging the fear, and persist. I will overcome.

I feel a surge of confidence. I don't even know how things could possibly fall into place to allow for my success. I feel that I will know once I get back. I need to get back. I want to get back. I feel eager.
I calm myself with the assurance that I can't rush. I need to stay composed and confident.

Despite my thoughts having been flustered, I feel more at ease now. I have an overwhelming sense of courage. The fear is still present, but I don't mind it. Courage cannot exist without fear.

I lie on the hotel bed and stare at the ceiling. My mind feels clearer suddenly. The thoughts are ceasing. All I hear in my mind is the sound of my breath echoing back at me. It's soothing. My body now feels comforted like my mind.

I close my eyes without the worry of nightmares. I'm in control of my mind. Anything the dark corners of my mind can conjure up will be swiftly brushed aside. My brave soul is fully at ease.

Chapter 38

I wake to the smell of coffee. She's back. I think the night has passed. She hands me a coffee and sits by me.

"Here's some wake-up juice," she says.

I sit up in the bed and look at her in somewhat of a daze. I smile. I feel great.

"That was possibly the most restful sleep I've ever had," I say.

"I'd hope so," she responds. "When I got back last night, I thought there was maybe a corpse in the bed. You were that still and quiet. I didn't want to wake you, but I didn't manage to get a place of my own to rest, so I snuck into the bed. You didn't move or make a sound even once throughout the night. Heck, I've been up for a few hours. You've slept quite a long time."

Although I'm slightly unsettled by her having slept next to me, I still feel happy. I see my future unfolding, and I have the courage to take it head-on.

"So, you ready to go?" I ask.

"Jeez, aren't you eager," she says.

"We can lie around as long as you want," I say. "Just thought you might want to head out."

"Let me finish my coffee and I'll drive on over to the next stop," she says.

"Awesome," I respond. "I feel full of energy. I'm going to head outside and do some exercise. Once you say the word, I'm hopping in the car."

Chapter 39

We arrive at a warehouse on the outskirts of the city limits. This is just outside where the protected area ends. The warehouse itself appears well protected with a tall, barbed wire wall and small watchtowers. The lights are on, and it is clearly operational.

We get past the gate and enter the reception area at the entrance. I take a seat as I let her speak to the receptionist. After a couple minutes, she walks over and takes a seat beside me. After a brief moment of silence, an old man comes in to greet us. He is dressed in a suit and tie and appears to be walking with a limp. He looks at her and says, "You look just like your mother!"

She smiles and gets out of her seat. She approaches the man and gives him a hug. She then says, "You look a bit different than in your pictures."

"Those pictures are old," he says. "Just like me."

After a brief moment of levity, his smile fades and he says, "Come. There's a conference room on the first floor."

We follow him into the conference room and take seats across from him at the table.

"What brings you all the way across the country?" he begins.

"We're trying to get to Boston," she responds.

Her saying those words seems to hit him hard. He looks grim. "We don't make those trips anymore," he responds.

Looking disappointed, she says, "But you're known for transporting goods across regions that people don't cross anymore. That's how your business took off."

The old man stands up and lifts his leg onto the table. He lifts the pantleg to reveal that he has a fake leg.

"It's too dangerous," he says. "We haven't been that way in over a year. We've lost people. I've lost my leg. I've already decided to have my company liquidated to cover the expenses from the tragedy of our last trip. We're not making any more deliveries. This business was never meant for the transportation of people anyway. You'd need a military escort, and to that, I say good luck."

Now visibly shaken, she stands from her seat, leans on the table, and says, "Have you seen this country? I know I have! I have driven all over it! Society is on the brink of collapse! Farms are suffering and are producing less and less! Soon, people won't be able to feed themselves! Anarchy reigns in much of the country, and two-thirds of the population has died in the past ten years!" She takes a deep breath and says, "The man next to me has given me hope that the misery can all end."

The old man across from us looks saddened and now looks away. He then asks, "Why did you leave? What's so important in Boston?"

"My family," I say.

He looks at me and sighs. His eyes twinkle with empathy. He then turns his gaze to her and asks, "How's he going to help save us?"

"He's a military operative who's been to the source of all this madness," she responds. "Out west, they don't believe in his knowledge, but I do. What they think doesn't matter though. Dad hooked me up. I had a much better life than most people on the West Coast due to my connections. Working for high-ranking government officials has its benefits and I have been using those to our advantage. I've just hit a bit of a roadblock and need some help."

The old man laughs and says, "Those bureaucratic positions are a joke these days. There are no more elections. The supposedly biggest and mightiest of them just hid away in their fortress over in D.C. while the rest of the city burned. Every nearby city had all their people desert them. Those that didn't died. New York City, Baltimore, Philadelphia. They are all gone. They gave too much credit to their overlords in Washington and suffered the consequences. As soon as things get tough, they abandon their people, whom they convinced they'd be there for. That dependence ruined such a large part of this country. As you should know, I was there. I saw it all unfold in person. And I was an actual elected official. I left D.C. out of disgust in myself and those around me. Your father was never any different. Don't rely on them."

After his angry rant comes silence. She's visibly hurt.

Seeing the tear roll down her face, he calms himself and says, "I'm sorry. I went too far." He looks down at himself and looks back at us. "I don't know if I can believe the fellow next to you can help what is already destroyed. I'm not sure that I could ever understand how we mend a fractured world. Then, again, I could never understand how this world became fractured in the first place. I can see that my ignorance shouldn't blind me from hope. I can't give up on hope. I can see you haven't. And for that, I trust you. I'll make the trip one last time. But you can't come. I'll bring him, but I want you to stay here in Buffalo until I return. I don't want to risk your safety."

"I'm coming," she says firmly. "I need to see this through. He wants to see his family before he does what is necessary, and I need to help wherever I can. I'll do anything to bring the old world back."

"Such confidence in your voice," he says. "You almost sound like a politician. You probably get it from your father. The main difference between you and a politician, though, is I truly believe you mean what you say. Unlike a typical politician, your voice is spoken through your heart." He smiles and says, "You can come along, but I will not compromise your safety. Leave your heroism for when I'm not looking after you."

"Don't worry. This guy is a hardened navy SEAL," she says as she grabs my arm.

"I had SEALs work for me," he says. "Not all of them have returned from these trips. Especially the last one. These are unique times. Unpredictable things can happen, and there is no way to prepare for them. Understand that. SEAL or no SEAL, this is dangerous."

Chapter 40

We find a small, cozy, sit-down restaurant to grab a meal while we wait for the old man to make the preparations for the trip. We're expecting to leave at nightfall. It's strange to think about, but nightfall has new meaning. With the everlasting twilight filling the sky, night falls around 7 p.m. It's about what we see on a clock and not what we see in the sky.

After we get seated and begin looking at the menu, I decide to ask a serious question. "Are you sure about this?"

"About what?" she asks.

"About making this journey," I respond. "This seems like we won't be able to circumnavigate danger this time. There is a chance that we won't return. Are you really sure you want to risk that?"

"I'm coming because I care about this country, about humanity. If I can help you in any way, I truly have no choice," she says.

After a moment of silence, I ask, "What ever happened to the other people you said you knew, the other people who wanted to help? You mentioned that back in San Francisco."

"That's somewhat of a sore subject," she says. "They did help where they could. Although they decided to stay in San Francisco…They believe in you. They believe this world can be saved. They still have that hope. That being said, they weren't willing to make the trip through even the safest parts of the journey. Fear has taken over. It's the instinct of self-preservation."

"Something you clearly lack," I respond.

"I want to do this for the same reason you fought for this country. You value others over yourself. We think like that because this isn't about us. It's about everybody. I don't want people to live in fear. People need to have control over their lives, their destiny, without a higher being oppressing the way they live. I want to help return hope to the world. Hope for the future." She says this all so eloquently.

"It all seems so ridiculous in retrospect. How can someone have that impact on the world? I still don't know if it's possible," I say. After a brief sigh, I say "All right then, let us represent hope and end this."

We actually have a nice time enjoying the meal. It's the best meal I've had since the hotel in San Francisco. I can feel the love and passion put into the creation of our meals. It makes me happy. Throughout the meal, we get lost in irrelevant discussion that is more lighthearted. Topics of old media and foreign foods. It's nice to talk about things that don't carry the weight of the world. I almost forget about the state of the world outside.

Unfortunately, all good things must come to an end. We have to leave the restaurant, and I see the purple sky again. I feel a pit in my stomach get deeper every time I acknowledge it. I feel sick.

As we get back to the warehouse, we are greeted with an enormous reinforced semitruck. The old man hops out and says, "All your stuff is already loaded up. We're headed for Troy, close to New England. There's an outpost there. After that, the terrain gets tricky, and we'll have to use ATVs with small trailers."

Then, a huge dog comes running towards the guy, and he promptly starts patting the dog and rubbing behind its ears. He then says, "This is my buddy. He's going to be accompanying us for the trip. He's very familiar with the route we'll be taking. Come on, we should get going."

Chapter 41

We sit comfortably in the trailer of the truck as the old man drives. There are no windows, and we are accompanied by the man's dog. The dog is resting its face in her lap as she strokes the top of its head. Everything is quiet for quite some time. Peaceful.

Eventually, the tranquility is interrupted as the road feels quite bumpy. We start to get tossed around. I can hear what sounds like creaking from sticks or logs as if we're driving through a lumber yard. The old man's voice resonates through the trailer from a speaker. "Sorry back there. I'm having some difficulty here. If you're wondering what we're running over, it's not something I want to tell you two, but rather something I need to tell you two. This truck is beefed-up for a reason. It's to get through unwanted obstacles. In this case, obstacles that are deciding to move in the way. They're trying to stop an unstoppable force and are getting plowed through. There's a lot more of these things than I remember." I can hear his nervous breathing as he pauses for a moment. "There are giant rodent things strung together like centipedes…Their undersides are just teeth made from ribs. I've seen them before. They can rip right through flesh like papier-mâché. Like land piranhas. If you see a squirrel, it runs away. If you see one of these things, it's coming for you. They have no sense of self-preservation. The thought of them made me reluctant to do this for you guys. I've had nightmares about my leg getting torn to shreds. Occasionally, you'll see them fighting with one of those things that looks like people parts mashed together. They do nothing but fight and destroy. You two need to understand what you're getting into.

Please just give this a second thought. After the next safe zone, you won't have the protection of this truck. The terrain is too rough. The area has been wrecked with earthquakes and rips in the earth. Things could get much more personal on the next part of the journey."

The old man's shocking descriptors sound shocking, but I have grown desensitized. Even my companion brushes the thoughts away with her determination as she remains stone faced through the old man's words.

The rest of the trip to Troy is a bumpy one. The man lets us know when we arrive, and we hop out the back of the trailer. The sight of the truck from the outside is a horror show. It's covered in dried blood and flesh. Some spots are still moist with recent roadkill.

When we are finally able to pull our eyes away from the tractor trailer, we look at the outpost we've arrived in. Hardly anyone is here. It's truly just an outpost, not meant for civilian living. It's just a secured checkpoint for travel.

We get some rest and prep for the rough path forward. There's no backing down. I don't care about the danger. I just want to see my family one last time before it may be too late. I need to know if they are okay. My mind is filled with hope despite the obstacles. My family is giving me that hope. I need to let them know I'm all right. I want them to be happy. I want them to feel the hope I feel. I need to say my goodbyes. Goodbyes aren't easy, but in my line of work, they've gotten used to it. Who am I kidding? It never gets easy. But seeing them could give me the edge I need to push forward into the unknown and give me something more to fight for.

I have to admit, sleep is not my priority for the night. I can't really tell how much time has passed since I left California.

With the exception of a couple stops, I've hardly slept at all. My mind is too alert.

This night is no different. When I awake from my brief sleep, I hear my two companions arguing with each other. He's trying to stop her from making the trip. I honestly don't want her to go either. This is far too dangerous to justify helping a stranger see their family, people she has no personal connection to. But she's as stubborn as they come. Maybe the most stubborn woman to have existed. I admire her unwillingness to give up. Despite that fact, I still think she's making the wrong decision. There's clearly no talking her out of this.

We set up the bikes and supplies. The man gave us ATVs, but he has opted for a motorbike with a sidecar for his dog. We'll have loaded weapons with us at all times. This is it. I'm almost there.

Chapter 42

Our vehicles of choice are electric. They make very little noise as we travel the difficult terrain. That being said, we are not completely silent, and I am still worried about what little noise we are making. I just have to reassure myself that the old man that is guiding us knows what he's doing. He's made many trips in the past and has the experience needed.

After some time, we arrive at a canyon that certainly didn't exist ten years ago.

"The path forward is down," says the man. "It's too dangerous to stay above ground. The longer we are above the ground, the more likely we are to be noticed by hostile creatures. Not only do we have to worry about the creatures in the dense wooded areas, but as you may have noticed, the land is covered in fractures that can be lethal to fall into. The path down leads to a maze of caves. It appeared a couple of years back. I've been through those caves dozens of times. These caves are quite large and aren't too difficult to traverse. It's weird because they almost seem man-made."

"I've seen areas like this before in San Francisco and even the Middle East," I say. "I've only experienced bad things when I go in these places. They have a reputation for people not coming back. It's shocking to hear you've used them so many times in the past."

"I said this is less dangerous; I never said this path was free of danger," the old man responds. "These tunnels come out near Worcester, and there is another outpost there. The rest of the trip should be easy from there."

We're so close. I don't know that we should be going this route. She hasn't said a word in a long time. It's unusual. I reluctantly follow the man down into the depths.

We arrive at the bottom without an issue, but as soon as we stop, she bolts into the cave ahead. The dog chases after her.

The old man jumps up and stops. He puts his hand on his head and says, "This is what I was afraid of. This place just calls to people." He then briskly goes in after her. After a brief moment of hesitation, I follow in pursuit.

We don't have sight of her, but we can hear the dog barking as it chases her. We follow the noise. This all happened too fast, and in the panic of the moment, we neglected to grab any decent source of light, leaving most of our supplies back at our vehicles. All we have to illuminate the dark tunnel are our flashlight attachments on our rifles.

As we run, the old man begins to lag far behind as he struggles with his prosthetic. "I won't forgive myself if I lose that girl! People who act like this don't typically get found!" he yells.

We come to where this cave ends and intersects another at an almost perfect ninety-degree angle. We can turn right or left, but the dog's barking sounds like it is coming from both directions. The man catches up, as I am not willing to make a decision. As he's about to reach me, I yell for him to take the shorter way to the left and I'll head down to the right. We both reach a turn in the tunnel at about the same time.

As the old man turns his corner, I turn back to him as I hear him yell, "Found you!" He then lets out a horrified scream as he falls backwards. I sprint back over to him as fast as possible. His screams quickly intensify. There is a fleshy dog with many heads and deformed appendages. It is smothering him and ripping his flesh with its boney, open body cavity.

I get on one knee and fire horizontally to hit just the beast. As my bullets rip through the many heads, they quickly become immobilized. But the rest of the creature is still moving as if a separate entity. The ribs of the creature are piercing the man's body and contorting him as if trying to consume him. In less than a second after my realization, I hear loud crunching from the man's back echo through the cave. His pained screams have stopped. I proceed to shoot the thing until no part of it moves. I get a bit closer to see if either the old man or creature is still alive. Neither is.

The lack of silence strikes me. The dog is still barking. I continue back down the other end of the cave towards what I have determined to be the source. I see her. I've caught up to them. She is still, just staring at a wall in a dead end. The dog is continuing to bark at her. I pat the dog on the head to get it to calm down, but it keeps barking. When I look back to her, I realize the dog isn't barking at her. It's barking at the wall she's staring at.

I walk over to her, grab her by the shoulders, look in her eyes, and then yell, "Why did you run off?"

In a small, scared voice, she says, "I don't know…I don't know…I don't know…"

Then, the wall at the dead end begins to crack. The cracks slowly widen. Suddenly, the wall crumbles and a hole opens up. It grows to the size of the tunnel. Beyond the hole lies a pitch-black tunnel, seemingly unpierced by my flashlight.

Everything starts to feel off. I feel like I'm falling. My fingers simultaneously feel like thin strands of straw and yet large sausages. Everything feels simultaneously slow yet sped up. My ability to feel myself and time are unexplainably warped. I feel the onset of panic. My thoughts begin to cross and melt into incomprehensive sound.

She looks at the opening and begins to walk towards it. I gather myself enough to react. I leap in front of her, feeling like I'm in a cave on the moon, and yell, "Stop!"

She stops and begins to cry. "I'm sorry!" she exclaims. "I don't know what I'm doing. I don't know what's happening. I shouldn't have convinced him to take this route. We should've gone around like he wanted. We could've been in Boston. You could've seen your family. They're alive. I didn't want to tell you. Yet I didn't care. I didn't want you to see them. I just wanted you to finish all of this. Bring back my world!"

She speaks fast in sobs through a broken voice. She's finally telling me the truth. My mind is still too flustered to fully comprehend the gravity of what she's saying. As I stand between her and the abyssal darkness, the shock makes me stumble back a few steps into the darkness. The cave opening shuts in front of me as soon as I enter. I'm cut off and trapped in the total darkness of a new cave.

Part 5

Chapter 43

I am surrounded by thick darkness and deafening silence. I see nothing. I hear nothing. I can't even hear the beats of my own heart. I try to step forward, but I am unable to. I can't move at all. Something is stopping me. I finally manage to locate my hands and drag them across the surface in front of me that I appear to be pressed against. It feels like a wall. I try to step back, but I stay in place. There is air beneath my feet, yet I do not fall. I push against the wall with my hands, and my head emerges from its depths. I see light. I stand on the wall to realize I can't tell which way is up. The wall must be the ground; I just can't feel the pull of gravity. My head is much too light. It's like I'm a magnet in space. The ground is very soft.

I fall back down unexplainably. I lie there and let out a deep breath as if it were the first time I had breathed in a long time. I feel like I'm sick in bed and don't want to get back up. I don't like having to get up when I feel so tired. I should be used to it by now, but it feels like that will never happen. I need to get out of bed or I'll be late. They don't like having to drive me when I miss the bus.

It'll be a long day. My brothers and I will be performing reconnaissance. We've learned the location of a terrorist leader. The lowlife is highly likely to be the man responsible for planning the deaths of over a hundred people.

After spending much of our time on the ground, we have determined the number of people at the suspect's compound. All are heavily armed. The target never leaves the premises. As night falls, we approach the compound. We take out the patrols and enter the building. To my group's surprise, the place is loaded with explosives. I thought we knew about this already. Regardless, we proceed to go around the complex and incapacitate the other terrorists. We split after clearing the first floor. I warn everyone to watch for traps and to be extra cautious and slow. I tell them to be weary of every step. I really want to drill it in their heads.

We split, and the upstairs is quickly covered. I radio the guys in the basement to see if they respond, but I hear nothing back. They didn't respond to my earlier warnings. I'm worried that they have been taken by a terrible fate. My partner and I rush into the basement only to walk into a living nightmare. It is the grizzliest sight I have ever seen. The basement is a booby-trapped torture chamber with mutilated men, women, and children. My own guys are before me, split in half on the floor. The thought that these people tortured nearby villagers makes me ill. We should have gone to the other side of the tunnel and done this in reverse. It would have been easier coming from the city entrance. Then, I hear an explosion of noise and darkness.

I wake up in my bed at home in a cold sweat. I've been having this nightmare regularly. I keep telling myself I couldn't have done anything more. I didn't know what I do now, but my desire to correct the past plagues me. It's like I feel I should've saved them.

That's when I hear a strange noise coming from my parents' room. It sounds like a monster. I reach up to the doorknob and slowly open the door to get out of the car. I need to make sure those people are all right. The car looks wrecked. I kick in the window and get into the car. The children are drowning. It's freezing and I can barely get my thoughts together. I quickly swim to the back of the bus to try to open the door. It just won't budge. I stare back at the children struggling to survive. They stop moving one by one. Then, everything opens. I escape out the back and approach my parents' bed. The noise is gone. Something sticks its hand out from under the bed and tries to grab my ankle. I jump and attempt to crawl up onto the bed. Long, scraggly hands bend up from beneath the bed and envelop me. I am getting dragged down. I scream for as loud as I can, hoping my parents will save me. I slowly lose sight of the light as I am dragged deeper under the bed until I see nothing at all.

Chapter 44

In the black emptiness, time stops. I am forced to calm myself down. I purge all thoughts from my mind. As I sit in a meditative state, my mind slowly begins to return to me. I open my eyes. My sight is blurred by tears. Nothing here is real. I need to gain control. I dry my eyes to see that I'm back in the cave. Not the cave I was just in, but rather the beautiful crystal cavern I left upon returning to the real world.

She isn't here. I need to gather my thoughts and remember what I'm doing. I have to control my surroundings. How did he do it? I still have the notebook! The bag I did manage to grab has what I need most. It still feels as heavy as it was for a different journey than the one I have found myself in. I take a look in my bag. It doesn't appear to have much in it. In fact, it suddenly feels quite light. All that I see in the bag is the notebook and journal. I just realized the weapon I strapped to myself is missing. I turn the bag upside down to see if anything else is in it, but only the notebook and journal fall out. As I watch them hit the ground, I look back at my hands and see that the bag has vanished.

When the journal hit the ground, it sprang open. I see writing in it. It didn't have anything in it before. It was forced open after being confiscated from me only to reveal nothing. Now, it is laden with writing.

I pick it up and look for somewhere to sit. I see no comfortable spot in the cave. As I continue to look, a chair appears in the middle of the large cave opening, as if my desire for a chair summoned one straight out of the cave floor. The deity must still be around. I look around and shout "Where are you!" I receive no answer.

My heart sinks when I realize it could be the evil man toying with me. Does he like to play with his prey before pouncing? I run out of the cave into the eternal twilight of unreality. There, I look around sporadically for either entity with no avail. Am I truly alone? Is it just me? Did I make the chair? Where did all of my things go?

I am far from comfortable with this situation. I wasn't prepared to come back yet. Now, I have the paranoia that I can't find a solution to the problem facing reality. Without thinking, I sit down, and I am seated in a very comfortable chair in the middle of nowhere. I'm in the middle of a plain of purple dirt and mostly dead vegetation. It came out of nothing. Did I make it? It's like my subconscious knew it would be there.

I shake off the confusion and decide the journal deserves my attention at this moment. The problem is the twilight of this world is too dim to read comfortably. Just as I begin to read, everything begins to get brighter. The whole landscape lights up. I look into the deep purple sky to see an enormous moon illuminating everything. There is not a cloud in the sky. There are also no stars. Like clockwork, as the thought floats through my mind, I start to notice twinkles in the sky. The sky is becoming more and more vibrant as I stare. The beauty of the sky is dumbfounding. It's as if you were to look into the sky on a clear night hundreds of miles from the light pollution of civilization. My awe slowly fades as my attention returns to the journal. Its contents are waiting to be revealed to me.

Chapter 45

<u>Entry 1:</u>

I haven't gotten a clue as to where I am. I don't know how long it's been. I'm glad I can now write down my experiences like I would do at my bedside. It's something that makes me feel comfortable. Reminds me of home.

<u>Entry 2:</u>

It's been quite some time. I have felt nothing but loneliness. I'm scared I will never see anyone again. I want to see my family. My beautiful wife and daughter. I want to smell the fields. Feel the warm breeze. See the stars and the blue sky. I'm trapped. I will do anything to feel their touch just one last time. I don't want to abandon them. We hardly make ten bucks a month sometimes. I was going to use my education to make things better. How will they survive? Come to think of it, in all the time I've been trapped in an expansive cage, I haven't needed anything. I don't feel hungry or thirsty no matter how far I've wandered. Am I already dead? Have I entered purgatory? Has God abandoned me?

<u>Entry 3:</u>

I have given it thought. The urge to abandon hope has disappeared. I have seen nothing in this place until this journal. I found one of my desires. That knowledge gives me a warm feeling inside. I can feel the ground beneath me, and I see the sky above my head. It means I still have my feet and mind about me. If I can find a journal to write in, what else can I discover?

<u>Entry 4:</u>

My heart is filled with joy. This is no purgatory nightmare any longer. My wife has been here as well. I have

finally found someone! The only thing that could make me happier is being reunited with our daughter. Now is not the time to be sad; it is the time to rejoice. The world around us has become so much more uplifting since I found her. I almost feel like we are back home. Plants have begun to sprout, and I see green. I see a vibrant blue sky and white clouds. The sun has shown itself, and I feel its warmth on my skin.
Entry 5:

The world has begun to feel unsettling once again. The absence of our daughter hurts us deeply. The world remains somewhat uncanny as well. The sun has not set at all. Day never ends. Nevertheless, we have persevered. We have wandered into green meadows and fertile fields near a large pond and decided to settle.
Entry 6:

My wife is worrying me. She doesn't act quite like I remember. She has quickly become happy and outgoing to an uncomfortable degree. It's as if she is oblivious to our life from before and may be content with remaining here. I'm a bit paranoid that I've gone crazy and that none of this is real. That my wife may still be in the real world. Could I have succumbed to death, and could this be a trick of the devil?
Entry 7:

I've begun to have these episodes. I see and experience things that I shouldn't. I hate to admit it, but I have felt my mind start to fade. The memories of my daughter have been blurry. After confessing to my wife, she showed me the most bittersweet sight. Never before has such immense happiness been met by equal sadness. I saw her on the other side. Our little girl. She's grown. Now with a new family. One she made on her own. We missed her grow up. How could we have been gone for so long? It's an absolutely heart-wrenching sight. My wife tells me we can be angels watching over her. She'll teach me how.

<u>Entry 8:</u>

My rage will not be matched. This world is full of deceit. I have been hoodwinked by an imposter. I knew it all along, but I didn't want to believe it. I thought I was with the woman I loved. She taught me how to peek into the real world. In doing so, she began her own demise. My wife never came to this place. She lived on for many years after I left and has since passed on to the real afterlife. The imposter had the skill to see into the real world all along and withheld the skill from me in fear of what I would discover. She was right to have that fear. She was wrong to trust I would ever love her. I have learned I was kidnapped. I need to get back to what's real. Little does she know, I have learned much more than she was able to teach. I have built a fortress in the appearance of a manor. I needed no materials. My mind was enough. I keep her at bay, as she has little power here. I will find a way out of the delusion concocted by the demon.

<u>Entry 9:</u>

I have seen more faces appear in this place. More demons have come to trick me. I will fall for no more deception. Anyone who attempts to impede my progress in leaving this world and destroying that cretin will be locked in my dungeon. I have felt my power grow. Nothing can stop me from breaking through to reality. My research has showed me how to abduct anything from the real world like that evil shapeshifter had done to me. My attempts to send things into the real world have unfortunately not had the desired results. I still have some ways before I am reunited with my daughter.

My hope has been lost. It has been a long time since my last entry. I have watched my daughter grow old. It saddens me to say, I have also witnessed the untimely ends of my grandchildren. My daughter was unable to continue the family. She also received an end that came all too soon. The illness was hard to watch. I can no longer bear the burden of watching the life of anyone. All that comes is death. This is my last entry. I can't carry the burden of memory anymore. I will focus on my research. Writing has comforted me, and my research will make a fine replacement. I will continue to learn in what new ways I can manipulate the world about me. So much could never be possible in the real world. I need to reinvent myself. I need to become more. Yet returning to the real world remains a desire as well. Maybe I can do both. There must be a way to combine both worlds so I can return with power.

Chapter 46

The man's brief entries have given me a new perspective on him. On this place. I can't allow myself to fall onto the path he took. Unfortunately, the journal doesn't quite help me in my approach with the unstable man. He has such vast power accumulated from his time here. I don't have time to learn like he did. I don't even know how much time has already passed. Then, there was that shapeshifting entity. I believe I know what that was. I am not as fortunate to have such a mentor to give me an advantage.

I have no choice but to push forward regardless. I have to believe in my mind and its connection to this world. That man may be smart and powerful, but his mind is old and frail. It has deteriorated beyond any point of reasoning.

I must persist. I have risked my life in the past for the greater good, and I will not tremble at this adversity. Although, I do not fear death as much as I fear failure. Failure is simply not an option. I need to confront him for this last time. And this is where the true problem is revealed. How do I even find him?

I look around at my surroundings and see nothing different. Nothing as far as my eyes can see. I'm nowhere. I need to be somewhere. All I can do is remember the last time I saw him. Forget the fear. Remember everything about that location. The large estate and the rolling fields, the garden, the beautiful sky, and that man. In my desire to return to that area, the memories all vividly flood my mind.

Very suddenly, faster than my brain can process. I'm there. I willed the location to me. I am standing exactly where I met that man. It looks distorted, as if things have changed. It all feels off.

I can't believe it worked. I can't believe how easy it was. The unease of my surroundings and the shock of it all floors me. I take a seat, as my legs feel numb and my head light. Having entered the lion's den doesn't help my unease. This is all supernatural. In my path forward, I have entered the true unknown unable to tell what will happen next. I can't have such fear. I need a clear mind. I have power. I need to use it.

As I look about. I see no sign of the man. I feel a bit more confidence. Somewhat peaceful. My whole body is now light. It's like a dream. I walk out of the garden and towards the manor. Things feel different, like details are missing or changing. I can't quite put my finger on it. I feel like I'm floating on water as I move. As I walk, I feel the air as if I'm swimming through it.

I need to find the man and confront him. I have to try to de-escalate before our interaction becomes aggressive. I honestly don't know that an aggressive approach would have any beneficial result for me. I don't know if I could be capable to overpower him. I can't have fear. I need to search for him.

Looking back at the garden, it's not as pretty as I thought. The more I look at it, the more unsettled I feel. It looks out of focus, like a mirage that isn't actually there. Could this just be from the crumbling of a man's broken mind? Maybe my encounter with him won't be as dire as I thought.

I look all over for that man but find nothing. I see nothing in the fields. Nothing outside at all. I head towards the front door and open it. I let myself into the huge entranceway and give a loud call for him. I will open myself up if needed. I just need to see him. But no matter how much I call, I get no response. There was no trap waiting for me. Nothing at all. I look in the kitchen, the hallways, rec room, library, upstairs. Nothing. I open every door in the house, revealing repeated bedrooms. There is an attic, but I find it more likely that he'd be in the basement, creating more monsters or conducting wretched experiments. Maybe he's as far down as his study.

"Experiments?" I hear a voice from behind me say. I was unaware I was saying my thoughts out loud. "I don't need experiments. My research is complete. I'm surprised you returned. I like your place. It's close, but certainly not homey." I slowly turn around in shock. That fear I've suppressed so well has now swelled in my mind. "What?" I say in confusion. "This place? My place?"

"Your imitation of my sanctuary is shameful. It leaves much to the imagination. And of course, such a large creation within this world was easy to notice. Your thoughts are so loud. Did you really want me to find you so easily? If you are so complicit, I'd love to use you for new research. I'm interested in learning about minds that have been so greatly affected by this world. Yours is the only one I know of. Unfortunately, I have more pressing matters to attend to for the time being. I'll leave you as a side project after I accomplish my current goal. And don't worry, I won't be making the same mistake I made from the last time we met. I've learned to treat you special from now on. Your new prison will be far more difficult to escape. It was quite fun to make. Even if you make it out, it will likely be at a time you will no longer be of concern to me. 'Til we meet again." He gives me a bow, and in an imperceivable instant, I'm back in that nightmare room where he imprisoned me so long ago.

Chapter 47

As I collect myself, the dread of many nightmares inhibits my mind, and I instinctively run to the door. Unexpectedly, the door opens. I stop in my tracks. This did not happen last time. As I stand there, I calm myself. I need my mind with me if I'm going to comprehend my situation. I look into the hall and suddenly realize there is no hall. I am staring into another bedroom.

I can't waste time with the man's mind games. I must be smart and get this world to bend to me as it does to him. I close the door and shut my eyes. I remember the hallway. I know what lies beyond this door. I try to picture the whole wall missing before me and that the bedroom has a gaping exit leading to the hallway. With full belief in myself, I step forward through what was the doorway with my eyes closed. Shockingly, I walk into nothing. I open my eyes and see that the wall has disappeared, but I am not standing in the hall. I am standing in the other bedroom. I just took two bedrooms and turned them into one giant bedroom with two of everything. There is still no way out.

I can feel my mind slip more and more as I interact with this world. I break. I can't do this. I run to a wall and begin scratching at the walls. My desire to tear down the walls fills me with unnatural strength. My fingers dig deep into the wall, and the wall falls before me. They all fall and crumble into nothing. My eyes are perplexing me as I look into infinity. I see beds as far as my eyes are able to see. The bedroom is copied endlessly. My madness tells me to run. I run and run but get nowhere. Everything is the same. I look to my feet. The floor! I must get rid of the floor! Before I even bend down to rip it apart, the floor disappears beneath my feet. My gut floats up into my mouth as I fall endlessly between furniture in a white void.

I need to collect myself. Otherwise, madness will be my downfall. I shut my eyes. I take a deep breath. I picture ground beneath my feet. I still feel like I'm falling no matter how hard I put my mind to it. I open my eyes and look down. Very suddenly, I spot a dark pit directly below me. I sling into it at a high velocity. I fly right into a corridor and am shot down most of the hallway before the ground meets me. I skid along my back and hit the end of the corridor.

Realizing I'm unharmed, I stand up and brush myself off. I look around to see that I've done it. I've escaped the room. I'm standing inside a hallway connected to the bedrooms. I smile as I feel a wave of self-fulfillment come across my body. But I can't get cocky. I need to find the man that trapped me and find a way to turn the tables on him.

I run to the stairs leading down to the first floor, only to have that good feeling leave me. I'm still trapped. The stairs go down to another hallway. It's not matching the manor's layout. This is not right. The next hallway is half as wide as the one I just ran down. With few options, I run down the stairs to the next hallway. As I look down the hallway, I see it tapers and gets thinner. I look back to the stairs I came down and see they are now gone. Instead, there is just a gap. Looking into the gap, I can see below and above the floor I'm on. I can see adjacent floor, tangential floor, and floors that do not have proper geometry. The hallways seem to twist and have various sizes of width and length. There are other stairways, many untraversable or just leading to nowhere. No ceiling is opaque.

I decide to proceed down the thin hallway. I cannot see the end of it, and it doesn't appear to taper completely closed. I get far enough down the hall that I need to turn sideways to proceed farther. It gets to a point where I do not believe it's worth proceeding through the squeeze, and I decide to turn back. I try to move back towards the way I came. I can't. The walls have pinched me, and I cannot move. I can't even turn my head to look behind me. I need to leave. This can't be what stops me. These walls need to be spread farther apart. They must. The pressure of the walls on my body suddenly ceases, and the walls separate to a dramatic extent. I now feel small in a hall I was once too big for. Moving down the hall now makes me feel like a rat scurrying across the floor. Then, a trapdoor opens underneath my feet, and I fall into a slide that twists upside down and brings me the reverse hallway on the underside. This floor lacks any sort of normal walls, as it is lined with mirrors. There are no doors. This is just a warped funhouse attraction at this point. My reflection is warped in the mirrors. Not only that, I actually feel myself warping. The odd feelings I've had before are physically occurring. My fingers are simultaneously thick and thin as I stare down at my hands. My thoughts are loud. I hear them and they're too loud. I can't think over the sound of my own thoughts. Where do I go?

I manage to ascend corkscrew steps to another floor. I go down this floor's hallway, then up another floor. I go down the hallway, then up. I go down, then up. The air is thick. The lights are now so bright, yet the corners of the hall stay so dark. I can't breathe.

I stop immediately in my tracks. I'm not getting anywhere. I'm just getting more lost. More unsettled. More confused. More distressed. I close my eyes and breathe deep. I know what I'm doing. I'm here with purpose. I can't forget that purpose. I can't fail. I look back at the funhouse the man created for me with some more clarity. I can't do this right now. I still need help. I was foolish to have sought him out. Rational decisions are hard to make in this place. I know who can help. But first, I need to get out of here. Continuing to be toyed with is wasting time. My mind wasn't fully with me. Now it is.

I picture walking through that pretty cave once again. The cave where I met her. I need her help. Just like that, the funhouse blinks out of existence and I'm in that cave. I breathe a sigh of relief. I can feel it. I'm out of that trap. I could have done this the whole time. I just needed to find my mind. The problem is, I can't be sure that this is the same cave I last saw her in. It looks like it, but it could be a copy from my mind like that manor. Taking a closer look around with a more solid frame of mind, nothing is off here. I feel that this is indeed the same cave. I don't believe the human mind can replicate anything this well. This has to be it. But where is she? Right as the question pops into my mind, I see a figure before me. It's her.

"Thank goodness. I thought..." As I begin talking, I have the realization that she's not right. I can just tell. She looks just how I remember her showing herself, but it doesn't fit right. My feeling is confirmed with her bare reaction. My mind brought a false figure to me because I desired it. This place keeps trying to confuse me.

I don't know what I should do. Then, I think about that last interaction I had with her. I try to remember every detail and walk through it in my head. I start to feel something suck me backwards. I felt this the last time I spoke with her. I do not fight the feeling. I think I know what's happening. I can't help but to want it to happen.

Chapter 48

It's dark. I can't see anything. I feel off balance. I shuffle my feet forward in the darkness, hoping to feel a wall. I kick something at my feet. I feel around for whatever it was and feel a gun. It has a light attachment. I turn it on to reveal I'm back in the cave. The cave I was in back in the real world. I think this was one of our guns. I can't tell if this is more of my mind's creations or if I'm really back. I don't feel truly back for some reason. Nevertheless, I can't abandon my task. I have to make sure I stay in unreality no matter my desire to leave it. I need to find her. I need to confront that man.

I appear to be at the dead end of the cave, so I move in the one direction I can. I don't get far before I hear some strange crunching noises. As I approach the sound, what appears to be natural light guides my way. I exit the cave to the sight of a dog. The very same dog that accompanied us to the death pit. He appears weak and hungry. I can easily see his ribs. He's chewing on something. Looks like a large bone. As I approach, the dog makes hostile growls. I can tell they are out of fear. I get close and he smells me. He calms down and lets me pet him. Looking closer at what he's chewing on, it's hard to tell, but the bone appears to be a human femur. I scan our surroundings and spot a nearby corpse. Most of the flesh has long been stripped away. I recognize the clothing on the dead body. It's the girl.

I drop to my knees as I feel a punch to my gut so fierce I vomit. I can't look at it. The dog approaches me in what appears to be an attempt to console me. He whimpers, and I embrace him firmly.

This is real. I don't want to believe it. I shouldn't be here. I need to get back. I feel my grief replaced with rage. I let go of the dog and yell out my frustration. My shout causes the ground beneath my feet to shake and rocks tumble down. The ground doesn't cease. Some strange creatures crawl out of cracks in the walls and seemingly from under dislodged boulders. They approach. The dog is on guard and growling aggressively. One amalgamation launches towards me, and I grab hold of it with no fear. I begin to pound on it. It tries to pierce me with its outward bones, but my skin appears impenetrable. I hear a whimper behind me. As I look back, the dog is being shredded. I look away and express the pain I feel onto this abomination. I pound it until it is nothing more than pulp on the crevice floor. The floor is shaking more aggressively. The creature feasting upon the dog is crushed by a landslide behind me. I don't flinch. I don't care. I have no fear.

A boulder falls on top of me. I do not move. The boulder moves around me. This isn't real. This is sick and twisted but not real. I calm myself. I clear my mind. I allow my body to feel light, and I begin to float in the air. I ascend from the crevice and allow it to close back up beneath me.

Everything looks as if I'm back, but I'm not. I can feel my influence over unreality growing, but it still isn't helping me find those I seek.

I feel hope slip. I have no idea what I'm doing. My newfound power isn't enough. I can't help but desire to be home. I don't want any of this. I never wanted this burden. I want to see my family. I want there to be a family waiting for my arrival. I just don't know anything anymore. And so, I sit in the middle of a forest beneath a deep purple sky, longing for home.

Chapter 49

I'm in my bed. The same bed I would have been in if I had managed to get back home after my final deployment. It feels just as I remember. I roll over and sit at the side of the bed. I look around the room at all the memories. I hear something walking in the hallway just outside my room. I do not hesitate and walk over to the door and slowly open it. It's my mother, heading towards the bathroom. She turns towards me, and her aged face turns white. She silently walks over to me and puts her hands on me. She then grabs me in a tight embrace and begins loudly weeping. She is sobbing uncontrollably. My dad walks out into the hallway and says in complete shock, "I…I don't believe it."

I begin to embrace my mother back and join her in the emotional breakdown. I guess this is real. When did I get back? Time just doesn't feel right to me. How did I get to my room in the real world? I don't get it. I suddenly feel an absence of feeling as the situation is now overwhelming to my mind.

Even after my mother regains some control over herself, she continues to hold on to me for the next half-hour, as she is convinced that I would disappear again if she lets go. We head downstairs to the living room, and my dad makes us all some tea. I have to explain my return and hope they believe me. Surprisingly, it doesn't take much. They believe every word I say as if it were gospel. From what they reveal to me, in the brief time I have been gone again, strange impossibilities have been happening. Things that I could expect from the other world. Their knowledge of the monsters isn't surprising, but what has surprised me is that the country's communications are mostly back, and tremors have ceased. Stranger yet, truly bizarre events have been witnessed regularly, as if people's nightmares are beginning to come to life. There are new monsters murdering people, and they are far different from the amalgamations of that man. The occurrences are becoming increasingly common even in safe zones. People are going missing more and more.

The last thing my parents tell me is where my living nightmare begins. The U.S. president was publicly executed on nationally broadcasted television. The American government is in shambles, and it is now the shell of a shell. Before committing the terrible act, the executioner claimed he would make everything better before flaying the president alive. This executioner is said to have mystical powers that can control the very fabric of reality.

It just can't be. He succeeded.

Chapter 50

I sit in shock. Motionless. The world has come to its end. That man has the world in his grasp as he sits on a throne in the capital of the strongest nation on the planet. Now that it's happened, I feel a calm I've never felt before. My mind has expanded beyond this mortal coil.

Unreality has spread into reality. They are almost one and the same. That evil is the only other mind aware. If I do nothing, the end to everything is inevitable. I need to prove to myself I can control this world like that man. The only way this could have happened is if she's here. He brought the creator of unreality into reality.

As the realization flows through my head, I look down at my hands. They're sweating. I concentrate on the perspired water and watch it collect into my hand. I lift it into the air. There is a small droplet of water floating before my eyes. I take the salt out of the sweat. Then, I make it disappear. It took no effort. I can do it.

I stand straight up and give my parents long and firm hugs. I tell them both I love them and that I will see them again very soon. In the very next instant, my eyes are gazing upon the White House.

Chapter 51

D.C. looks like a nuke landed. Many buildings are falling apart and in ruin. The Washington Monument is broken. Debris is everywhere. The decayed dead litter the landscape. Yet, the White House remains immaculate.

There are large, hairless amalgamations of what can be described as some of the largest land animals mashed together into a humanoid figure ten feet tall. It appears there are many of these creatures patrolling the area. As I stand out in the open, I am immediately spotted. Their movements are unclear, as if blurring through existence. These creatures that should not exist propel gurgling roars from their orifices. I feel no fear from the sight of these monsters. I proceed up to the entrance of the White House and simply ignore them. They do not hesitate to attack. They cannot do anything to harm me. As soon as they make contact with me, their bodies fall apart into their original components, then cease to exist.

That man knows I'm here. I can feel his presence, and he can feel mine. He storms out of the building before I can enter. The sight of me enrages him.

"How dare you!" he screams. "You cannot escape your fate! No one has!"

He raises his arms as if conducting an orchestra and floats off the ground. The ground rumbles and all the debris rattles. Corpses and limbs shoot out of the dust and meld together, forming a flesh monster with uncountable appendages. It is twice as tall as the now-broken monument. Upon its incarnation, the creature tries to grab me, but as it picks me up, its limbs quickly begin to flow into a viscous slime that pours onto the ground. It tosses me into the reflecting pool nearby. The pool is filled with blood, and I lay submerged for a moment. The very next instant, I'm shooting through that abomination's giant mass, causing it to explode into millions of meat chunks. I continue on toward the man. I grab him by the throat, and we crash through the White House.

I remain calm. He is consumed by rage and fear. I have him pinned.

"Fool!" he shouts. "You cannot end me!" He then vanishes from my grasp and appears before me.

He pauses for a brief moment to collect himself. "It seems we have reached an impasse," he says. "There is nothing you can do to stop me, but I will figure out a way to stop you!"

"And then what?" I ask. "What will you do with a world where you are the god? You've had it and done nothing but plot and do evil. Nothing has changed after coming here. You are a destroyer more than a creator. You think you can collect yourself, but you are fractured. You may have been a human at one point, but you have become a demon psychopath who lacks any remnant of his past self. What would your family think if they were around to see what you have become?"

"How dare you!" the man yells, flustered. "You know nothing!"

"Your past is something you have forgotten," I respond.

The man yells and disappears. His voice booms throughout the bleak sky and thick air. "The next time we meet, you will fear me!"

Chapter 52

He's right. Best-case scenario, I become an immovable object to his unstoppable force. It all cancels out in the end. I can't truly stop him from doing what he wants. I can't defeat him. Not on my own. The world twisting and mixing with unreality clouds the mind.

Time moves differently. Thoughts are slow. I have to hold on to what little reality there is left. Reality is still being lost but still persists to some extent. It's warped but still here. Just like my mind. His mind, on the other hand, has been lost a long time ago. He only has his power here for one reason. She's here. That deity from another world has entered this one. It's just as he wanted. Just as he needed. I need to find that manifestation. He must have locked her away somewhere. A trap for her consciousness. Her presence is what allows unreality to take over reality. But where is she being held?

The thought gives me a strange feeling. It's a strong connection to unreality. My mind and unreality have been interwoven. I have been corrupted. Or have I corrupted it? No, neither.

As I feel through unreality, it comes to me. She is unreality. I'm already connected to her. It's as if I can absorb knowledge from her fabric of unreality. It must be how I've been learning so quickly. I just haven't realized it. This is my lead. I can follow the trail of her mind. She was able to detect me in my first visit to her domain. Anyone that enters her domain must have the potential to connect with unreality and use her power with no limit other than from the limited knowledge of how to do so. The knowledge has come somewhat naturally to me.

Following a trail to the source of unreality isn't coming simple to me. I can feel it, but I can't quite pinpoint the direction.

I sit atop the roof of the White House and stare into the surrounding wastes. I look into the destruction of what was once a large city. I may not have thought it was a great city before the apocalypse, but this takes it to a level of dread that cannot be described. This sight in particular saddens me to my core.

I can't let such sights distract me from my goal. I breathe deeply and try to clear my mind. I need to focus on my connection to her.

And so, I sit. I sit for minutes. Ten minutes. I sit. Hours must pass. I am relaxed. I lose all focus on the destruction in reality, but rather the destructive unreality. I feel it. I feel her. I know where she is.

Chapter 53

This is it. I have arrived where this all can end.

Before me sway countless amber waves of grain. They sway without sound. No wind. The air is still like a vacuum void of all sound, yet they are alive. Most of the surroundings are covered in a deep darkness as if light refuses to touch much of the earth. In contrast, the sky is a dull gray, but quite bright. The silhouette of a small farmstead can be seen along the horizon. The environment gives an awful feeling of nothing. I can tell what this once was. This is the real location. A place that man once called home.

As I approach his original domain, the cellar door calls to me. As their presence in my sight grows, they slowly begin to open. I do not hesitate. I descend down the cellar stairs into a dark abyss. In the void I have found myself in, I see her. She has remained in the form she found most endearing, a mother to life.

She is curled up as if asleep and prone. She quickly takes notice of my approach. She stands, unable to move any closer. She is in pain. She feels sorrow and regret. The fabric of her being is no longer her own, and she feels it tearing her apart. Her inherited human emotion has overtaken her. The tears coming from her eyes present a clear picture. She is happy yet terrified. I am here to comfort her. The man has no knowledge of my presence. I'm able to approach unimpeded. I break her physical barrier, and we embrace strongly.

"I am here," I whisper.

She embraces me back even harder, as if she were a lost child reuniting with their parent. In that moment, something begins to happen. I feel less of me. I feel more of her. She is more real now than ever before. We briefly share existence as one. Our consciousnesses unite together as one. I feel her past. The endless loneliness. The ability to stare back into a time without a start. I see into eternity.

Suddenly, she pushes me away. The tears have cleared from her face, leaving but a smile.

"You've done it," she said. "I know what to do now. For just a moment, I was human. The mind of a human is truly remarkable. I understand my power."

She opens a portal back to her world without needing to make a movement and says, "I have halted the end. The man has no power. He will soon realize it. He is in the master bedroom above. I do not want to risk being near him again. As our minds merged, you must have discovered why. I am allowing you to remain a conduit of my power. Please talk to him. I truly do still love him. Return to me once you've done what I've asked. I'm already incapable of thanking you, but please, this is the last thing I will ever ask of you."

I know now that everything is over. The world will continue to exist. I should be overcome with relief, but I feel nothing. Just calm. I turn away and proceed out of the abyss to have my final confrontation with that attempted bringer of the end.

Chapter 54

I walk into the modest farmhouse. I hear the footsteps of its inhabitant. It's him. He's pacing around his living area. He suddenly stops to look at a large empty picture frame sitting on a small table. He reaches out and strokes it. I proceed towards him.

"Do you remember what that was a picture of?" I ask.

He turns around abruptly in surprise and shouts, "How? Be gone!"

He gestures as if he were trying to cast me away with magic. He stands in shock and confusion. A moment passes before he staggers backwards in fear and asks, "Why are you still here? Why can't I leave? What trickery have you bestowed upon me?"

"There are no tricks," I respond. "You are mortal once again. The true divine being of the world you've taken advantage of has been enlightened. She's in control now. I've freed her and now you have lost."

His knees fall weak. He has to lean on a chair to not fall over. He then sits down as he shows signs of losing his balance. His eyes are darting back and forth as if watching the room spin.

"I feel ill," he says. Then, he stares at me and says, "Kill me! Do it! Get this over with! I can't take this!"

I sit nearby and say, "No."

There is a short moment of silence before I ask, "What was in that picture?"

"I don't know," he says, somewhat despondent.

"Well, it seems to be calling out to you in some way," I say as I stand back up. I take the picture from the table and hand it to him.

He stares at it in silence.

"Do you know where you are?" I ask.

"This was once my home," he says. "When I came back, it was gone. So, I brought it back."

"You're missing some details," I say as I point to the picture he's now holding.

He doesn't respond.

I sigh deeply before continuing. "What do you remember…from before. Before getting trapped."

He still says nothing.

This farmstead we sit in is much smaller than his from the other world. I stand up and walk around. Two bedrooms. A room with a small bed and a room with a large one. I stand inside the doorway of the room with the large bed and ask, "This is your room, I assume?"

He still remains silent.

I move over to the other room and ask, "This was your daughter's, right?"

Before I get my last word out, I hear him mutter to himself "daughter." He drops his head into his hands and despondently says, "I don't remember her face."

I hand over his journal. He is shocked just from the sight of it. Nonetheless, he opens it once I hand it to him. He begins reading and looks agitated. As he finishes reading each page, he rips it out and throws it.

"How dare she," he says. "How dare she! My family!"

He then looks up to me, hardly able to keep his composure. Holding back tears, in a cracked voice he says, "I was betrayed."

"She's full of remorse," I say. "She loves and cares for you. She didn't realize the damage her actions would cause. She wanted to be human like us. She wanted to have someone to love, like you. It's hard to forgive, but she is sorry."

"She destroyed my world," he says. "So I wanted to destroy hers and rebuild mine, but it appears I was only ever good at destruction. After coming back to this world, I realized it could never truly be mine, but I tried nonetheless. I shouldn't have…What have I done?"

He begins to break down and bawl. As the tears stream from his face, he asks his final question.

"I've become worse than her, haven't I? She was my personal angel of destruction, yet I am everyone else's! I've created horrors that no human should be capable of! Kill me already! I deserve it! No creation of mine is as big a monster as the one I have become!"

I walk over to him and rest my hand on his shoulder.

"I won't kill you," I say. "I'd like for you to come with me and recompense."

He calms down and looks into my eyes, then nods. We then vanish into the abyss below the house to speak with the deity one last time.

Chapter 55

The man is unfazed by our descent. When he looks up, his eyes meet hers as she stands between worlds.

She looks caringly into his eyes and says, "I need to make amends. I am responsible for the tragedy bestowed upon you. I am equally responsible for your actions. Your mind has not been well."

"I deserve no pity," he tells her. "I accomplished nothing in what has felt like a lucid dream. I have committed terrible sins. Only now do I feel human again. I remember now. I appreciate your sentiment, but I cannot forgive you nor myself. Please, rid yourself from this world and let me rot."

She sees his misery and steps back into our world. She walks towards him and gives him an embrace. As they comfort one another, the world fills the void. We are back outside. The sun is shining in the bright blue sky. I hear the birds chirping and bugs buzzing. The man looks different. As she lets him go, he steps back to look at his hands. He feels his face. Somehow, he seems more human. Then, a magical sound rings through the air and grabs his attention. It's the laughter of a child. He is visibly shaken and begins to wipe the tears from his face.

"It's my daughter!" he says with a smile. "Is this real?"

The deity nods her head and says, "I have split reality in two. This reality has been returned to the moment you left it. Please, live a happy life for me."

He embraces her one last time before walking back towards his farmhouse to see his family.

Even I'm in shock. In my awe, she grabs my hand and looks me in the eyes. I see the cosmos. I see infinite beauty.

Then, I'm back with my brothers. They're here with me. Alive. In the comfort of our old barracks.

She has vanished from my sight, but I hear her voice ring in my head.

"This is the other side of the split. Live a great life for me. May we meet again."

One of my brothers in arms gives me a pat on the back unaware of my experience and asks, "You coming? Let's go!" A briefing is about to begin. We are all about to go on a very important mission. This time, we'll do things right.